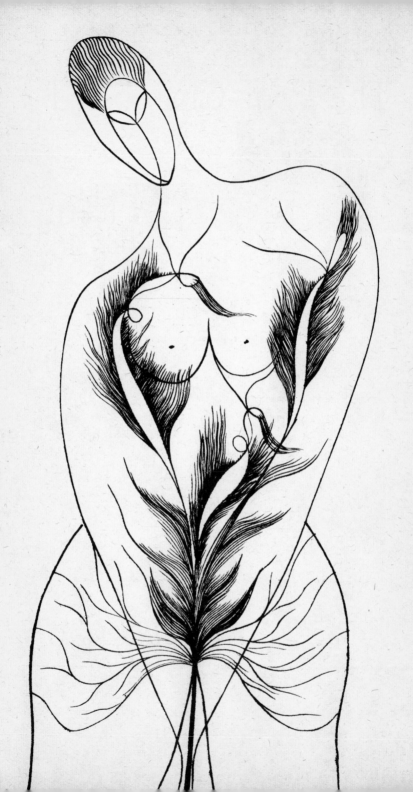

The Four-Chambered

Heart

By Anaïs Nin

THE **SWALLOW PRESS** INC.

CHICAGO

Published by
The Swallow Press Incorporated
1139 South Wabash Avenue
Chicago, Illinois 60605

This book is printed on 100% recycled paper.

ISBN 0–8040–0121–9
LIBRARY OF CONGRESS CATALOG CARD NUMBER 66–6825

The guitar distilled its music.

Rango played it with the warm copper color of his skin, with the charcoal pupil of his eyes, with the underbrush thickness of his eyebrows, pouring into the honey-colored box the flavors of the open road on which he lived his gypsy life: thyme, rosemary, oregano, marjoram, and sage. Pouring into the resonant box the sensual swing of his hammock hung across the gypsy cart and the dreams born on his mattress of black horsehair.

Idol of the night clubs, where men and women barred doors and windows, lit candles, drank alcohol, and drank from his voice and his guitar the potions and herbs of the open road, the charivaris of freedom, the drugs of leisure and laziness.

At dawn, not content with the life transfusion through catguts, filled with the sap of his voice which had passed into their veins, at dawn the women wanted to lay hands upon his body. But at dawn Rango swung his guitar over his shoulder and walked away.

Will you be here tomorrow, Rango?

Tomorrow he might be playing and singing to his black horse's philosophically swaying tail, on the road to the south of France.

Toward this ambulant Rango, Djuna leaned to catch all that his music contained, and her ear detected the presence of this unattainable island of joy which she pursued, which she had glimpsed at the party she had never attended but watched from her window as a girl. And like some lost voyager in a desert, she leaned more and more eagerly toward this musical mirage of a pleasure never known to her, the pleasure of freedom.

"Rango, would you play once for my dancing?" she

asked softly and fervently, and Rango stopped on his way out to bow to her, a bow of consent which took centuries of stylization and nobility of bearing to create, a bow indicating the largesse of gesture of a man who had never been bound.

"Whenever you wish."

As they planned for the day and hour, and while she gave him her address, they walked instinctively toward the river.

Their shadows walking before them revealed the contrast between them. His body occupied twice the space of hers. She walked unswerving like an arrow, while he ambled. His hands trembled while lighting her cigarette, and hers were steady.

"I'm not drunk," he said, laughing, "but I've been drunk so often that my hands have remained unsteady for life, I guess."

"Where is your cart and horse, Rango?"

"I have no cart and horse. Not for a long time. Not since Zora fell ill, years ago."

"Zora?"

"My wife."

"Is your wife a gypsy, too?"

"Neither my wife nor I. I was born in Guatemala, at the top of the highest mountain. Are you disappointed?

That legend was necessary to keep up, for the night club, to earn a living. It protects me, too. I have a family in Guatemala who would be ashamed of my present life. I ran away from home when I was seventeen. I was brought up on a ranch. Even today my friends say: 'Rango, where is your horse? You always look as if you had left your horse tied to the gate.'—I lived with the gypsies in the south of France. They taught me to play. They taught me to live as they do. The men don't work; they play the guitar and sing. The women take care of them by stealing food under their wide skirts. Zora never learned that! She got very ill. I had to give up roaming. We're home now. Do you want to come in?"

Djuna looked at the gray stone house.

She had not yet effaced from her eyes the image of Rango on the open road. The contrast was painful and she took a step backward, suddenly intimidated by a Rango without his horse, without his freedom.

The windows of the house were long and narrow. They seemed barred. She coud not bear yet to see how he had been captured, tamed, caged, by what circumstances, by whom.

She shook his big hand, the big warm hand of a captive, and left him so swiftly he was dazed. He stood bewildered and swaying, awkwardly lighting another cigarette, wondering what had made her take flight.

8

He did not know that she had just lost sight of an island of joy. The image of an island of joy evoked by his guitar had vanished. In walking toward a mirage of freedom, she had entered a black forest, the black forest of his eyes darkening when he said: 'Zora is very ill.' The black forest of his wild hair as he bowed his head in contrition: 'My family would be ashamed of the life I lead today.' The black forest of his bewilderment as he stood about to enter a house too gray, too shabby, too cramped for his big, powerful body.

Their first kiss was witnessed by the Seine River carrying gondolas of street lamps' reflections in its spangled folds, carrying haloed street lamps flowering on bushes of black lacquered cobblestones, carrying silver filigree trees opened like fans beyond whose rim the river's eyes provoked them to hidden coquetries, carrying the humid scarfs of fog and the sharp incense of roasted chestnuts.

Everything fallen into the river and carried away except the balcony on which they stood.

Their kiss was accompanied by the street organ and it lasted the whole length of the musical score of Carmen, and when it ended it was too late; they had drunk the potion to its last drop.

The potion drunk by lovers is prepared by no one but themselves.

The potion is the sum of one's whole existence.

Every word spoken in the past accumulated forms and colors in the self. What flows through the veins besides blood is the distillation of every act committed, the sediment of all the visions, wishes, dreams, and experiences. All the past emotions converge to tint the skin and flavor the lips, to regulate the pulse and produce crystals in the eyes.

The fascination exerted by one human being over another is not what he emits of his personality at the present instant of encounter but a summation of his entire being which gives off this powerful drug capturing the fancy and attachment.

No moment of charm without long roots in the past, no moment of charm is born on bare soil, a careless accident of beauty, but is the sum of great sorrows, growths, and efforts.

But love, the great narcotic, was the hothouse in which all the selves burst into their fullest bloom . . .

love the great narcotic was the revealer in the alchemist's bottle rendering visible the most untraceable substances

love the great narcotic was the *agent provocateur* exposing all the secret selves to daylight

love the great narcotic lined fingertips with clairvoyance

pumped iridescence into the lungs for transcendental x-rays

printed new geographies in the lining of the eyes

adorned words with sails, ears with velvet mutes

and soon the balcony tipped their shadows into the river, too, so that the kiss might be baptized in the holy waters of continuity.

Djuna walked along the Seine the next morning asking the fishermen and the barge sailors for a boat to rent in which she and Rango might live.

As she stood by the parapet wall, and then leaned over to watch the barges, a policeman watched her.

(Does he think I am going to commit suicide? Do I look like someone who would commit suicide? How blind he is! I never wanted less to die, on the very day I am beginning to live!)

He watched her as she ran down the stairs to talk to the owner of Nanette, a bright red barge. Nanette had little windows trimmed with beaded curtains just like the superintendent's windows in apartment houses.

(Why bring to a barge the same trimmings as those of a house? They are not made for the river, these people, not for voyages. They like familiarity, they like to continue their life on earth, while Rango and I want to run away from houses, cafes, streets, people. We want to find an island, a solitary cell, where we can dream in peace together. Why should the policeman think I may jump into the river at this moment when I never felt less like dying? Or does he stand there to reproach me for slipping out of my father's house last night after ten o'clock, with such infinite precautions, leaving the front door ajar so he would not hear me leave, deserting his house with a beating heart because now his hair is white and he no longer understands anyone's need to love, for he has lost everything, not to love, but to his games of love; and when you love as a game, you lose everything, as he lost his home and wife, and now he clings to me, afraid of loss, afraid of solitude.)

That morning at five-thirty she had awakened, gently untangled her body from Rango's arms and reached her room at six, and at six-thirty her father had knocked on the door because he was ill and wanted care.

(Ali Baba protects the lovers! Gives them the luck of bandits, and no guilt; for love fills certain people and expands them beyond all laws; there is no time, no place for regrets, hesitations, cowardices. Love runs free and reckless; and all the gentle trickeries perpetrated to protect others from its burns—those who are not the lovers but who might be the victims of this love's expansion—let them be gentle and gay about these trickeries, gentle and gay like Robin Hood, or other games of children; for Anahita, the moon goddess, will then judge and mete out punishment, Mr. Policeman. So wait for her orders, for I am sure you would not understand if I told you my father is delightfully clear and selfish, tender and lying, formal and incurable. He exhausts all the loves given to him. If I did not leave his house at night to warm myself in Rango's burning hands I would die at my task, arid and barren, sapless, while my father monologues about his past, and I yawn yawn yawn . . . it's like looking at family albums, at stamp collections! Understand me, Mr. Police-man, if you can: if that were all I had, I would indeed be in danger of jumping into the Seine, and you would have to take a chill rescuing me. See, I have money for a taxi, I sing a song of thanksgiving to the taxi which nourishes the dream and carries it unbreakable, fragile but unbreak-able everywhere. The taxi is the nearest object to a seven-leagued boot, it perpetuates the reverie, my vice, my lux-ury. Oh, you can, if you wish, arrest me for reverie, vagabondage of the wildest sort, for it is the cell, the mys-terious, the padded, the fecund cell in which everything is born; everything that man ever accomplished is born in this little cell . . .)

The policeman passed by and did not arrest her, so she confided in him and found him rich with knowledge. He knew of many barges here and there. He knew one where they served fried potatoes and red wine to fisher-men, another where hobos could spend the night for five cents, one where a woman in trousers carved big statues, another one turned into a swimming pool for boys, an-other one called the barge of the red lights, for men, and beyond this one there was a barge that had been used by a troupe of actors to travel all through France, and there she might inquire as it was empty and had been deemed unsafe for long voyages . . .

It was anchored near the bridge, long and wide, with a strong prow from which hung the heavy anchor chain. It had no windows on the side, but a glass trap door on deck which an old watchman threw open for her. She descended a narrow and steep stairway to find herself in a broad room, with light falling from skylight windows, and then there were a smaller room, a hallway, and more small cabins on each side.

The large center room which had been used for the stage was still full of discarded sets and curtains and costumes. The small cabins which branched off on both sides had once been dressing rooms for the ambulant actors. They were now filled with pots of paint, firewood, tools, old sacks, and newspapers. At the prow of the barge was a vast room papered with glossy tarpaper. The skylight windows showed only the sky, but two openings in the wall, working like drawbridges on a chain, were cut only a few inches above water level and focused on the shore.

The watchman occupied one of the small cabins. He wore a beret and dark blue denim blouse like the French peasants.

He explained: "I was the captain of a pleasure yacht once. The yacht blew up and I lost my leg. But I can fetch water for you, and coal and wood. I can pump the water every day. This barge has to be watched for leaks. It's pretty old, but the wood is strong."

The walls of the barge curved like the inside of a whale belly. The old beams were stained with marks of former cargoes: wood, sand, stone, and coal.

As Djuna left, the old watchman picked up a piece of wood which held a pail at each end, hanging on a cord. He balanced it on his shoulders like a Japanese water carrier, and began to jump on his one leg after her, keeping a miraculous balance on the large cobblestones.

The winter night came covering the city, dusting the street lamps with fog and smoke so that their light dissolved into an aureole of sainthood.

When Djuna and Rango met, he was sad that he had found nothing to shelter them. Djuna said: "I have something for you to see; if you like it, it might do for us."

As they walked along the quays, as they passed the station through a street being repaired, she picked up one of the red lanterns left by the repair men, and carried it, all lit, across the bridge. Halfway they met the same policeman who had helped her find the barge. Djuna thought: he will arrest me for stealing a street lantern.

But the policeman did not stop her. He smiled, knowing where she was going, and merely appraised Rango's build as they passed.

The old watchman appeared suddenly at the trap door and shouted: "Hey, there! Who goes there? Oh, it's you, petite madame. Wait. I'll open for you." And he threw the trap door fully open.

They descended the turning stairway and Rango smelled the tar with delight. When he saw the room, the shadows, the beams, he exclaimed: "It's like the Tales of Hoffmann. It's a dream. It's a fairy tale."

Old grandfather of the river, ex-captain of a pleasure yacht, snorted insolently at this remark and went back to his cabin.

"This is what I wanted," said Rango.

He bent down to enter the very small room at the tip of the barge which was like a small pointed prison with barred windows. The enormous anchor chain hung before the iron bars. The floor had been worn away, rotted with dampness, and they could see through the holes the layer of water which lies at the bottom of every ship, like the possessive fingers of the sea and the river asserting its ownership of the boat.

Rango said: "If ever you're unfaithful to me, I will lock you up in this room."

With the tall shadows all around them, the medieval beams cracking above their heads, the lapping water, the mildew at the bottom, the anchor chain's rusty plaintiveness, Djuna believed his words.

"Djuna, you're taking me to the bottom of the sea to live, like a real mermaid."

"I must be a mermaid, Rango. I have no fear of depths and a great fear of shallow living. But you, poor Rango, you're from the mountain, water is not your element. You won't be happy."

"Men from the mountains always dream of the sea, and above all things I love to travel. Where are we sailing now?"

As he said this, another barge passed up the river close to theirs. The whole barge heaved; the large wooden frame cracked like a giant's bones.

Rango lay down and said: "We're navigating."

"We're out of the world. All the dangers are outside, out in the world." All the dangers . . . dangers to the love, they believed as all lovers believe, came from the outside, from the world, never suspecting the seed of death of love might lie within themselves.

"I want to keep you here, Djuna. I would like it if you never left the barge."

"I wouldn't mind staying here."

(If it were not for Zora, Zora awaiting food, awaiting medicines, awaiting Rango to light the fire.)

"Rango, when you kiss me the barge rocks."

The red lantern threw fitful shadows, feverish red lights, over their faces. He named it the aphrodisiac lamp.

He lighted a fire in the stove. He threw his cigarette into the water. He kissed her feet, untied her shoes, he unrolled her stockings.

They heard something fall into the water.

"It's a flying fish," said Djuna.

He laughed: "There are no flying fish in the river, except you. When you're in my arms, I know you're mine. But your feet are so swift, so swift, they carry you as lightly as wings, I never know where, too fast, too fast away from me."

He rubbed his face, not as everyone does, with the palm of the hand. He rubbed it with his fists closed as children do, as bears and cats do.

He caressed her with such fervor that the little red

lantern fell on the floor, the red glass broke, the oil burst into many small wild flames. She watched it without fear. Fire delighted her, and she had always wanted to live near danger.

After the oil was absorbed by the thick dry wooden floor, the fire died out.

They fell asleep.

The drunken grandfather of the river, ex-captain of a pleasure yacht, had lived alone on the barge for a long time. He had been the sole guardian and owner of it. Rango's big body, his dark Indian skin, his wild black hair, his low and vehement voice frightened the old man.

When Rango lit the stove at night in their bedroom, the old man in his cabin would begin to curse him for the noise he made.

Also he resented that Rango did not let him wait on Djuna, and he would mutter against him when he was drunk, mutter threats in apache language.

One night Djuna arrived a little before midnight. A

windy night with dead leaves blowing in circles. She was always afraid to walk alone down the stairs from the quays. There were no lights. She stumbled on hobos asleep, on whores plying their trade behind the trees. She tried to overcome her fear and would run down the steps along the edge of the river.

But finally they had agreed that she would throw a stone from the street to the roof of the barge to warn Rango of her arrival and that he would meet her at the top of the stairs.

This night she tried to laugh at her fears and to walk down alone. But when she reached the barge there was no light in the bedroom, and no Rango to meet her, but the old watchman popped out of the trap door, vacillating with drink, red-eyed and stuttering.

Djuna said: "Has Monsieur arrived?"

"Of course, he's in there. Why don't you come down? Come down, come down."

But Djuna did not see any light in the room, and she knew that if Rango were there, he would hear her voice and come out to meet her.

The old watchman kept the trap door open, saying as he stamped his feet: "Why don't you come down? What's the matter with you?" with more and more irritability.

Djuna knew he was drunk. She feared him, and she started to leave. As his rage grew, she felt more and more certain she should leave.

The old watchman's imprecations followed her.

Alone at the top of the stairs, in the silence, in the dark, she was filled with fears. What was the old man doing there at the trap door? Had he hurt Rango? Was Rango in the room? The old watchman had been told he could no longer stay on the barge. Perhaps he had avenged himself. If Rango were hurt, she would die of sorrow.

Perhaps Rango had come by way of the other bridge.

It was one o'clock. She would throw another stone on the roof and see if he responded.

As she picked up the stone, Rango arrived.

Returning to the barge together, they found the old watchman still there, muttering to himself.

Rango was quick to anger and violence. He said: "You've been told to move out. You can leave immediately."

The old watchman locked himself in his cabin and continued to hurl insults.

"I won't leave for eight days," he shouted. "I was a captain once, and I can be a captain any time I choose again. No black man is going to get me out of here. I have a right to be here."

Rango wanted to throw him out, but Djuna held him back. "He's drunk. He'll be quiet tomorrow."

All night the watchman danced, spat, snored, cursed, and threatened. He drummed on his tin plate.

Rango's anger grew, and Djuna remembered other people saying: "The old man is stronger than he looks. I've seen him knock down a man like nothing." She knew Rango was stronger, but she feared the old man's treachery. A stab in the back, an investigation, a scandal. Above all, Rango might be hurt.

"Leave the barge and let me attend to him," said Rango.

Djuna dissuaded him, calmed his anger, and they fell asleep at dawn.

When they came out at noon, the old watchman was already on the quays, drinking red wine with the hobos, spitting into the river as they passed, with ostentatious disdain.

The bed was low on the floor; the tarred beams creaked over their heads. The stove was snoring heat, the river water patted the barge's sides, and the street lamps from the bridge threw a faint yellow light into the room.

When Rango began to take Djuna's shoes off, to warm her feet in his hands, the old man of the river began to shout and sing, throwing his cooking pans against the wall:

> "Nanette gives freely
> what others charge for.
> Nanette is generous,
> Nanette gives love
> Under a red lantern"

Rango leaped up, furious, eyes and hair wild, big body tense, and rushed to the old man's cabin. He knocked on the door. The song stopped for an instant, and was resumed:

> "Nanette wore a ribbon
> In her black hair.
> Nanette never counted
> All she gave. . . ."

Then he drummed on his tin plate and was silent.
"Open the door!" shouted Rango.
Silence.

Then Rango hurled himself against the door, which gave way and tore into splinters.

The old watchman lay half naked on a pile of rags, with his beret on his head, soup stains on his beard, holding a stick which shook from terror.

Rango looked like Peter the Great, six feet tall, black hair flying, all set for battle.

"Get out of here!"

The old man was dazed with drunkenness, and he refused to move. His cabin smelled so badly that Djuna stepped back. There were pots and pans all over the floor, unwashed, and hundreds of old wine bottles exuding a rancid odor.

Rango forced Djuna back into the bedroom and went to fetch the police.

Djuna heard Rango return with the policeman, and heard his explanations. She heard the policeman say to the watchman: "Get dressed. The owner told you to leave. I have an injunction here. Get dressed."

The watchman lay there, fumbling for his clothes. He could not find the top of his pants. He kept looking down into one of the pant's legs as if surprised at its smallness. He mumbled. The policeman waited. They could not dress him because he would turn limp. He kept muttering: "Well, what do I care? I used to be captain of a yacht. Something white and smart, not one of these broken-down barges. I used to have a white suit, too. Suppose you do throw me into the river, it's all the same to me. I don't care if I die. I'm not a bad old man. I run errands for you, don't I? I fetch water, don't I? I bring coal. What if I do sing a bit at night."

"You don't just sing a bit," said Rango. "You make a hell of a noise every time you come home. You bang your pails together, you raise hell, you bang on the walls, you're always drunk, you fall down the stairs."

"I was sound asleep, wasn't I? Sound asleep, I tell you. Who knocked the door down, tell me? Who broke into my cabin? I'll not get out. I can't find my pants. These aren't mine, they're too small."

Then he began to sing:

> "Laissez moi tranquille,
> Je ferais le mort.
> Ma chandelle est morte
> Et ma femme aussi"

Then Rango, the policeman, and Djuna all began to laugh. No one could stop laughing. The old man looked so dazed and innocent.

"You can stay if you're quiet," said Rango.

"If you're not quiet," said the policeman, "I'll come back and fetch you and throw you in jail."

"Je ferais le mort," said the old man. "You'll never know I'm here."

He was now thoroughly bewildered and docile. "But no one has a right to knock a door down. What manners, I tell you! I've knocked men down often enough, but never knocked a door down. No privacy left. No manners."

When Rango returned to the bedroom, he found Djuna still laughing. He opened his arms. She hid her face against his coat and said: "You know, I love the way you broke that door." She felt relieved of some secret accumulation of violence, as one does watching a storm of nature, thunder and lightning discharging anger for us.

"I loved your breaking down that door," repeated Djuna.

Through Rango she had breathed some other realm she had never attained before. She had touched through his act some climate of violence she had never known before.

The Seine River began to swell from the rains, and to rise high above the watermark painted on the stones in the Middle Ages. It covered the quays at first with a thin layer of water, and the hobos quartered under the bridge had to move to their country homes under the trees. Then it lapped the foot of the stairway, ascended one step, and then another, and at last settled at the eighth, deep enough to drown a man.

The barges stationed there rose with it; the barge dwellers had to lower their rowboats and row to shore, climb up a rope ladder to the wall, climb over the wall to the firm ground. Strollers loved to watch this ritual, like a gentle invasion of the city by the barges' population.

At night the ceremony was perilous, and rowing back and forth from the barges was not without difficulties. As the river swelled, the currents became violent. The smiling Seine showed a more ominous aspect of its character.

The rope ladder was ancient, and some of its solidity undermined by time.

Rango's chivalrous behavior was suited to the circumstances; he helped Djuna climb over the wall without showing too much of the scalloped sea-shell edge of her petticoat to the curious bystanders; he then carried her into the rowboat, and rowed with vigor. He stood up at first and with a pole pushed the boat away from the shore,

as it had a tendency to be pushed by the current against the stairway, then another current would absorb it in the opposite direction, and he had to fight to avoid sailing down the Seine.

His pants rolled up, his strong dark legs bare, his hair wild in the wind, his muscular arms taut, he smiled with enjoyment of his power, and Djuna lay back and allowed herself to be rescued each time anew, or to be rowed like a great lady of Venice.

Rango would not let the watchman row them across. He wanted to be the one to row his lady to the barge. He wanted to master the tumultuous current for her, to land her safely in their home, to feel that he abducted her from the land, from the city of Paris, to shelter and conceal her in his own tower of love.

At the hour of midnight, when others are dreaming of firesides and bedroom slippers, of finding a taxi to reach home from the theatre, or pursuing false gaieties in the bars, Rango and Djuna lived an epic rescue, a battle with an angry river, a journey into difficulties, wet feet, wet clothes, an adventure in which the love, the test of the love, and the reward telescoped into one moment of wholeness. For Djuna felt that if Rango fell and were drowned she would die also, and Rango felt that if Djuna fell into the icy river he would die to save her. In this instant of danger they realized they were each other's reason for living, and into this instant they threw their whole being.

Rango rowed as if they were lost at sea, not in the heart of a city; and Djuna sat and watched him with admiration, as if this were a medieval tournament and his mastering of the Seine a supreme votive offering to her feminine power.

Out of worship and out of love he would let no one light the stove for her either, as if he would be the warmth and the fire to dry and warm her feet. He carried her down the trap door into the freezing room damp with winter fog. She stood shivering while he made the fire with an intensity into which he poured his desire to warm her, so that it no longer seemed like an ordinary stove smoking and balking, or Rango an ordinary man lighting wood with damp newspapers, but like some Valkyrian hero lighting a fire in a Black Forest.

Thus love and desire restored to small actions their large dimensions, and renewed in one winter night in Paris the full stature of the myth.

She laughed as he won his first leaping flame and said: "You are the God of Fire."

He took her so deeply into his warmth, shutting the door of their love so intimately that no corroding external air might enter.

And now they were content, having attained all lovers' dream of a desert island, a cell, a cocoon, in which to create a world together from the beginning.

In the dark they gave each other their many selves, avoiding only the more recent ones, the story of the years before they met as a dangerous realm from which might spring dissensions, doubts, and jealousies. In the dark they sought rather to give each other their earlier, their innocent, unpossessed selves.

This was the paradise to which every lover liked to return with his beloved, recapturing a virgin self to give one another.

Washed of the past by their caresses they returned to their adolescence together.

Djuna felt hersef at this moment a very young girl, she felt again the physical imprint of the crucifix she had worn at her throat, the incense of mass in her nostrils. She remembered the little altar at her bedside, the smell of candles, the faded artificial flowers, the face of the virgin, and the sense of death and sin so inextricably entangled in her child's head. She felt her breasts small again in her modest dress, and her legs tightly pressed together. She was now the first girl he had loved, the one he had gone to visit on his horse, having traveled all night across the mountains to catch a glimpse of her. Her face was the face of this girl with whom he had talked only through an iron gate. Her face was the face of his dreams, a face with the wide space between the eyes of the madonnas of the sixteenth century. He would marry this girl and keep her jealously to himself like an Arab husband, and she would never be seen or known to the world.

In the depth of this love, under the vast tent of this love, as he talked of his childhood, he recovered his innocence, too, an innocence much greater than the first, because it did not stem from ignorance, from fear, or from neutrality in experience. It was born like an ultimate pure gold out of many tests, selections, from voluntary rejection of dross. It was born of courage, after many desecrations, from much deeper layers of the being inaccessible to youth.

Rango talked in the night. "The mountain I was born on was an extinct volcano. It was nearer to the moon. The moon there was so immense it frightened man. It appeared at times with a red halo, occupying half of the sky, and everything was stained red. . . . There was a bird we hunted, whose life was so tough that after we shot him the Indians had to tear out two of his feathers and plunge them into the back of the bird's neck, otherwise it would not die. . . . We killed ducks in the marshes, and once I was caught in quicksands and saved myself by getting quickly out of my boots and leaping to safe ground. . . . There was a tame eagle who nestled on our roof. . . . At dawn my mother would gather the entire household together and recite the rosary. . . . On Sundays we gave formal dinners which lasted all afternoon. I still remember the taste of the chocolate, which was thick and sweet, Spanish fashion. . . . Prelates and cardinals came in their purple and gold finery. We led the life of sixteenth-century Spain. The immensity of nature around us caused a kind of trance. So immense it gave sadness and loneliness. Europe seemed so small, so shabby at first, after Guatemala. A toy moon, I said, a toy sea, such small houses and gardens. At home it took six hours by train and three weeks on horseback to reach the top of the mountain where we went hunting. We would stay there for months, sleeping on the ground. It had to be done slowly because of the strain on the heart. Beyond a certain height the horses and mules could not stand it; they would bleed through mouth and ears. When we reached the snow caps, the air was almost black with intensity. We would look down sharp cliffs, thousands of miles down, and we would see below, the small, intensely green, luxuriant tropical jungle. Sometimes for hours and hours my horse would travel alongside of a waterfall, until the sound of the falling water would hypnotize me. And all this time, in snow and wildness, I dreamed of a pale slender woman. . . . When I was seventeen, I was in love with a small statue of a Spanish virgin, who had the wide space between the eyes which you have. I dreamed of this woman, who was you, and I dreamed of cities, of living in cities. . . . Up in the mountain where I was born one never walked on level ground, one walked always on stairways, an eternal stairway toward the sky, made of gigantic square stones. No one knows how the Indians were able to pile these stones one upon another; it seems humanly impossible. It seemed more like a stairway made by gods, because the steps were higher than a man's step could encompass. They were built for giant gods, for the Mayan giants carved in granite, those who drank the blood of sacrifices, those who laughed at the puny efforts of men who tired of taking such big steps up the flanks of mountains. Volcanoes often erupted and covered the Indians with fire and lava and ashes. Some were caught descending the rocks, shoulders bowed, and frozen in the lava, as if cursed by the earth, by maledictions from the bowels of the earth. We sometimes found traces of footsteps bigger than our own.

Could they have been the white boots of the Mayans? Where I was born the world began. Where I was born lay cities buried under lava, children not yet born destroyed by volcanoes. There was no sea up there, but a lake capable of equally violent storms. The wind was so sharp at times it seemed as if it would behead one. The clouds were pierced by sandstorms, the lava froze in the shape of stars, the trees died of fevers and shed ashen leaves, the dew steamed where it fell, and clouds rose from the earth's parched cracked lips. . . . And there I was born. And the first memory I have is not like other children's; my first memory is of a python devouring a cow. . . . The poor Indians did not have the money to buy coffins for their dead. When bodies are not placed in coffins a combustion takes place, little explosions of blue flames, as the sulphur burns. These little blue flames seen at night are weird and frightening. . . . To reach our house we had to cross a river. Then came the front patio which was as large as the Place Vendôme. . . . Then came the chapel which belonged to our ranch. A priest was sent for from town every Sunday to say mass. . . . The house was large and rambling, with many inner patios. It was built of pale coral stucco. There was one room entirely filled with firearms, all hanging on the walls. Another room filled with books. I still remember the cedar-wood smell of my father's room. I loved his elegance, manliness, courage. . . . One of my aunts was a musician; she married a very brutal man who made her unhappy. She let herself die of hunger, playing the piano all through the night. It was hearing her play night after night, until she died, and finding her music afterward, which drew me to the piano. Bach, Beethoven, the best, which at that time were very little known in such far-off ranches. The schools of music were only frequented by girls. It was thought to be an effeminate art. I had to give up going there and study alone, because the girls laughed at me. Although I was so big, and so rough in many ways, loved hunting, fighting, horseback riding, I loved the piano above everything else. . . . The mountain man's obsession is to get a glimpse of the sea. I never forgot my first sight of the ocean. The train arrived at four in the morning. I was dazzled, deeply moved. Even today when I read the Odyssey it is with the fascination of the mountain man for the sea, of the snow man for warm climates, of the dark, intense Indian for the Greek light and mellowness. And it is that which draws me to you, too, for you are the tropics, you have the sun in you, and the softness, and the clarity. . . ."

What had happened to this body made for the mountain, for violence and war? A little blue flame of music, of art, from the body of the aunt who had died playing Bach, a little blue flame of restless sulphur had passed into this body made for hunting, for war and the tournaments of love. It had lured him away from his birthplace, to the cities, to the cafes, to the artists.

But it had not made of him an artist.

It had been like a mirage, stealing him from other lives, depriving him of ranch, of luxury, of parents, of marriage and children, to make of him a nomad, a wanderer, a restless, homeless one who could never go home again: "Because I am ashamed, I have nothing to show, I would be coming back as a beggar."

The little blue flame of music and poetry shone only at night, during the long nights of love, that was all. In the daytime it was invisible. As soon as day came, his body rose with such strength that she thought: he will conquer the world.

His body—which had not been chiseled like a city man's, not with the precision and finesse of some highly finished statue, but modeled in a clay more massive, more formless, too, cruder in outline, closer to primitive sculpture, as if it had kept a little of the heavier contours of the Indian, of animals, of rocks, earth, and plants.

His mother used to say: "You don't kiss me like a boy, but like a little animal."

He began his day slowly, like a cub, rubbing his eyes with closed fists, yawning with eyes closed, a humorous, a sly, upward wrinkle from mouth to high cheekbone, all his strength, as in the lion, hidden in a smooth form, no visible sign of effort.

He began his day slowly, as if man's consciousness were something he had thrown off during the night, and had to be recovered like some artificial covering for his body.

In the city, this body made for violent movements, to leap, to face a danger of some kind, to match the stride of a horse, was useless. It had to be laid aside like a superfluous mantle. Firm muscles, nerves, instincts, animal quickness were useless. It was the head which must awaken, not the muscles and sinews. What must awaken was awareness of a different kind of danger, a different kind of effort, all of it to be considered, matched, mastered in the head, by some abstract wit and wisdom.

The physical euphoria was destroyed by the city. The supply of air and space was small. The lungs shrank. The blood thinned. The appetite was jaded and corrupt.

The vision, the splendor, the rhythm of the body were instantly broken. Clock time, machines, auto horns, whistles, congestion caught man in their cogs, deafened, stupefied him. The city's rhythm dictated to man; the imperious order to remain alive actually meant to become an abstraction.

Rango's protest was to set out to deny and destroy the enemy. He set out to deny clock time and he would miss, first of all, all that he reached for. He would make such detours to obey his own rhythm and not the city's that the simplest act of shaving and buying a steak would take hours, and the vitally important letter would never be written. If he passed a cigar store, his habit of counter-discipline would be stronger than his own needs and he would forget to buy the cigarettes he craved, but later when about to reach the house of a friend for lunch he would make a long detour for cigarettes and arrive too late for lunch, to find his angry friend gone, and thus once more the rhythm and pattern of the city were destroyed, the order broken, and Rango with it, Rango left without lunch.

He might try to reach the friend by going to the cafe, would find someone else and fall into talk about book-binding and meanwhile another friend was waiting for Rango at the Guatemalan Embassy, waiting for his help, his introduction, and Rango never appeared, while Zora waited for him at the hospital, and Djuna waited for him in the barge, while the dinner she had made spoiled on the fire.

40

At this moment Rango was standing looking at a print on the bookstalls, or throwing dice over a cafe counter to gamble for a drink, and now that the city's pattern had been destroyed, lay in shambles, he returned and said to Djuna: "I am tired." And laid a despondent, a heavy head on her breasts, his heavy body on her bed, and all his unfulfilled desires, his aborted moments, lay down with him like stones in his pockets, weighing him down, so that the bed creaked with the inertia of his words: "I wanted to do this, I wanted to do that, I want to change the world, I want to go and fight, I want. . . ."

But it is night already, the day has fallen apart, disintegrated in his hands, Rango is tired, he will take another drink from the little barrel, eat a banana, and start to talk about his childhood, about the bread tree, the tree of the shadows that kill, the death of the little Negro boy his father had given him for his birthday, a little Negro boy who had been born the same day as Rango, but in the jungle, and who would be his companion on hunting trips, but who died almost immediately from the cold up in the mountains.

Thus at twilight when Rango had destroyed all order of the city because the city destroyed his body, and the day lay like a cemetery of negations, of rebellions and abortions, lay like a giant network in which he had tangled himself as a child tangles himself in an order he cannot understand, and is in danger of strangling himself . . . then Djuna, fearing he might suffocate, or be crushed, would tenderly seek to unwind him, just as she picked up the pieces of his broken glasses to have them made again. . . .

They had reached a perfect moment of human love. They had created a moment of perfect understanding and accord. This highest moment would now remain as point of comparison to torment them later on when all natural imperfections would disintegrate it.

The dislocations were at first subtle and held no warning of future destruction. At first the vision was clear, like a perfect crystal. Each act, each word would be imprinted on it to shed light and warmth on the growing roots of love, or to distort it slowly and corrode its expansion.

Rango lighting the lantern for her arrival, for her to see the red light from afar, to be reassured, incited to walk faster, elated by this symbol of his presence and his fervor.

His preparing the fire to warm her. . . . These rituals Rango could not sustain, for he could not maintain the effort to arrive on time since his lifelong habit had created the opposite habit: to elude, to avoid, to disappoint every expectation of others, every commitment, every promise, every crystallization.

The magic beauty of simultaneity, to see the loved one rushing toward you at the same moment you are rushing toward him, the magic power of meeting exactly at midnight to achieve union, the illusion of one common rhythm achieved by overcoming obstacles, deserting friends, breaking other bonds—all this was soon dissolved by his laziness, by his habit of missing every moment, of never keeping his word, of living perversely in a state of chaos, of swimming more naturally in a sea of failed intentions, broken promises, and aborted wishes.

The importance of rhythm in Djuna was so strong that no matter where she was, even without a watch, she sensed the approach of midnight and would climb on a bus, so instinctively accurate that very often as she stepped off the bus the twelve loud gongs of midnight would be striking at the large station clock.

This obedience to timing was her awareness of the rarity of unity between human beings. She was fully, painfully aware that very rarely did midnight strike in two hearts at once, very rarely did midnight arouse two equal desires, and that any dislocation in this, any indifference, was an indication of disunity, of the difficulties, the impossibilities of fusion between human beings.

Her own lightness, her freedom of movement, her habit of sudden vanishings made her escapes more possible, whereas Rango, on the contrary, had never been known to leave except when the bottles, the people, the night, the cafe, the streets were utterly empty.

But for her, his inability to overcome the obstacles which delayed him lessened the power of his love.

Little by little, she became aware that he had two fires to light, one at home for Zora, and one on the barge. When he arrived late and wet, she was moved by his tiredness and her awareness of his burdens at home, and she began to light the fire for him.

He loved to sleep late, while she would be awakened by the passing of coal barges, by foghorns, and by the heavy traffic over the bridge. So she would dress quietly and she would run to the cafe at the corner and return with coffee and buns to surprise him on awakening.

"How human you are, Djuna, how warm and human. . . ."

"But what did you expect me to be?"

"Oh, you look as if the very day you were born you took

one look at the world and decided to live in some region between heaven and earth which the Chinese called the Wise Place."

The immense clock of the Quai d'Orsay station which sent people traveling, showed such an enormous, reproachful face in the morning: it is time to take care of Zora, it is time to take care of your father, it is time to return to the world, time time time. . . .

As she knew how much she had loved to see the red lantern gleaming behind the window of the barge as she walked toward it, when Rango fell back into his habit of lateness, it was she who lit the lantern for him, mastering her fear of the dark barge, the drunken watchman, the hobos asleep, the moving figures behind the trees.

When she discovered how strong was his need of wine, she never said: don't drink. She bought a small barrel at the flea market, had it filled with red wine, and placed it at the head of the bed within reach of his hand, having faith that their life together, their adventures together, and the stories they told each other to pass the time, would soon take the place of the wine. Having faith that their warmth together would take the place of the warmth of the wine, believing that all the natural intoxications of caresses would flow from her and not the barrel. . . .

Then one day he arrived with a pair of scissors in his pocket. Zora was in the hospital for a few days. It was she who always cut his hair. He hated barbers. Would Djuna like to cut his hair?

His heavy, his brilliant, his curling black hair, which neither water nor oil could tame. She cut it as he wished, and felt, for a moment, like his true wife.

Then Zora returned home, and resumed her care of Rango's hair.

And Djuna wept for the first time, and Rango did not understand why she wept.

"I would like to be the one to cut your hair."

Rango made a gesture of impatience. "I don't see why you should give that any importance. It doesn't mean anything. I don't understand you at all."

If it were not for music, one could forget one's life and be born anew, washed of memories. If it were not for music one could walk through the markets of Guatemala, through the snows of Tibet, up the steps of Hindu temples, one could change costumes, shed possessions, retain nothing of the past.

But music pursues one with some familiar air and no longer does the heart beat in an anonymous forest of heartbeats, no longer is it a temple, a market, a street like a stage set, but now it is the scene of a human crisis reen-acted inexorably in all its details, as if the music had been the score of the drama itself and not its accompaniment.

The last scene between Rango and Djuna might have faded into sleep, and she might have forgotten his refusal to let her cut his hair once more, but now the organ grinder on the quay turned his handle mischievously, and aroused in her the evocation of another scene. She would not have been as disturbed by Rango's evasiveness, or his defense of Zora's rights to the cutting of his hair, if it had not added itself to other scenes which the organ grinder had at-tended with similar tunes, and which he was now recre-ating for her, other scenes where she had not obtained her desire, had not been answered.

The organ grinder playing Carmen took her back in-exorably like an evil magician to the day in her childhood when she had asked for an Easter egg as large as herself, and her father had said impatiently: "What a silly wish!" Or to another time when she had asked him to let her kiss his eyelids, and he had mocked her, or still another time when she had wept at his leaving on a trip and he had said: "I don't understand your giving this such impor-tance."

Now Rango was saying the same thing: "I don't understand why you should be sad at not being able to cut my hair any longer."

Why could he not have opened his big arms to her, sheltered her for an instant and said: "It cannot be, that right belongs to Zora, but I do understand how you feel, I do understand you are frustrated in your wish to care for me as a wife. . . ."

She wanted to say: "Oh, Rango, beware. Love never dies of a natural death. It dies because we don't know how to replenish its source, it dies of blindness and errors and betrayals. It dies of illnesses and wounds, it dies of weariness, of witherings, of tarnishings, but never of natural death. Every lover could be brought to trial as the murderer of his own love. When something hurts you, saddens you, I rush to avoid it, to alter it, to feel as you do, but you turn away with a gesture of impatience and say: 'I don't understand.' "

It was never one scene which took place between human beings, but many scenes converging like great intersections of rivers. Rango believed this scene contained nothing but a whim of Djuna's to be denied.

He failed to see that it contained at once all of Djuna's wishes which had been denied, and these wishes had flown from all directions to meet at this intersection and to plead once more for understanding.

All the time that the organ grinder was unwinding the songs of Carmen in the orchestra pit of this scene, what was conjured was not this room in a barge, and these two people, but a series of rooms and a procession of people, accumulating to reach immense proportions, accumulating analogies and repetitions of small defeats until it contained them all, and the continuity of the organ grinder's accompaniment welded, compressed them all into a large injustice. Music expanding the compressed heart created a tidal wave of injustice for which no Noah's Ark had ever been provided.

The fire sparkled high; their eyes reflected all its dances joyously.

Djuna looked at Rango with a premonition of difficulties, for it so often happened that their gaiety wakened in him a sudden impulse to destroy their pleasure together. Their joys together never a luminous island in the present but stimulating his remembrance that she had been alive before, that her knowledge of caresses had been taught to her by others, that on other nights, in other rooms, she had smiled. At every peak of contentment she would tremble slightly and wonder when they would begin to slide into torment.

This evening the danger came unsuspected as they talked of painters they liked, and Rango said suddenly: "And to think that you believed Jay a great painter!"

When she defended a friend from Rango's irony and wit it always aroused his jealousy, but to defend an opinion of a painter, Djuna thought, could be achieved without danger.

"Of course, you'll defend Jay," said Rango, "he was a part of your former life, of your former values. I will never be able to alter that. I want you to think as I do."

"But Rango, you couldn't respect someone who surrendered an opinion merely to please you. It would be hypocrisy."

"You admire Jay as a painter merely because Paul admired him. He was Paul's great hero in painting."

"What can I say, Rango? What can I do to prove to you that I belong to you? Paul is not only far away but you know we will never see each other again, that we were not good for each other. I have completely surrendered him, and I could forget him if you would let me. You are the one constantly reminding me of his existence."

At these moments Rango was no longer the fervent, the adoring, the warm, the big, the generous one. His face would darken with anger, and he made violent gestures. His talk became vague and formless, and she could barely catch the revealing phrase which might be the key to the storm and enable her to abate or deflect it.

A slow anger at the injustice of the scene overtook her. Why must Rango use the past to destroy the present? Why did he deliberately seek torment?

She left the table swiftly, and climbed to the deck. She sat near the anchor chain, in the dark. The rain fell on her and she did not feel it; she felt lost and bewildered.

Then she felt him beside her. "Djuna! Djuna!"

He kissed her, and the rain and the tears and his breath mingled. There was such a desperation in his kiss that she melted. It was as if the quarrel had peeled away a layer and left a core like some exposed nerve, so that the kiss was magnified, intensified, as if the pain had made a fine incision for the greater penetration of pleasure.

"What can I do?" she murmured. "What can I do?"

"I'm jealous because I love you."

"But Rango, you have no cause for jealousy."

It was as if they shared his illness of doubt and were seeking a remedy, together.

It seemed to her that if she said, "Jay was a bad

painter," Rango could see the obviousness of such a recantation, its absurdity. Yet how could she restore his confidence? His entire body was pleading for reassurance, and if her whole love was not enough what else could she give him to cure his doubt?

When they returned to the room the fire was low.

Rango did not relax. He found some books piled next to the wastebasket which she had intended to throw away. He picked them up and studied them, one by one, like a detective.

Then he left the ones she had discarded and walked to those aligned on the book shelf.

He picked one up at random and read on the fly leaf: "From Paul."

It was a book on Jay, with reproductions of his paintings.

Djuna said: "If it makes you happy, you can throw it away with the others."

"We'll burn them," he said.

"Burn them all," she said with bitterness.

To her this was not only an offering of peace to his tormenting jealousy, but a sudden anger at this pile of books whose contents had not prepared her for moments such as this one. All these novels so carefully concealing the truth about character, about the obscurities, the tangles, the mysteries. Words words words words and no revelation of the pitfalls, the abysms in which human beings found themselves.

Let him burn them all; they deserved their fate.

(Rango thinks he is burning moments of my life with Paul. He is only burning words, words which eluded all truths, eluded essentials, eluded the bare demon in human beings, and added to the blindness, added to the errors. Novels promising experience, and then remaining on the periphery, reporting only the semblance, the illusions, the costumes, and the falsities, opening no wells, preparing no one for the crises, the pitfalls, the wars, and the traps of human life. Teaching nothing, revealing nothing, cheating us of truth, of immediacy, of reality. Let him burn them, all the books of the world which have avoided the naked knowledge of the cruelties that take place between men and women in the pit of solitary nights. Their abstractions and evasions were no armor against moments of despair.)

She sat beside him by the fire, partaking of this primitive bonfire. A ritual to usher in a new life.

If he continued to destroy malevolently, they might reach a kind of desert island, a final possession of each other. And at times this absolute which Rango demanded, this peeling away of all externals to carve a single figure of man and woman joined together, appeared to her as a desirable thing, perhaps as a final, irrevocable end to all the fevers and restlessness of love, as a finite union. Perhaps a perfect union existed for lovers willing to destroy the world around them. Rango believed the seed of destruction lay in the world around them, as for example in these books which revealed to Rango too blatantly the difference between their two minds.

To fuse then, it was, at least for Rango, necessary to destroy the differences.

Let them burn the past then, which he considered a threat to their union.

He was driving the image of Paul into another chamber of her heart, an isolated chamber without communicating passage into the one inhabited by Rango. A place in some obscure recess, where flows eternal love, in a realm so different from the one inhabited by Rango that they would never meet or collide, in these vast cities of the interior.

"The heart . . . is an organ . . . consisting of four chambers. . . . A wall separates the chambers on the left from those on the right and no direct communication is possible between them. . . ."

Paul's image was pursued and hid in the chamber of gentleness, as Rango drove it away, with his holocaust of the books they had read together.

(Paul, Paul, this is the claim you never made, the fervor you never showed. You were so cool and light, so elusive, and I never felt you encircling me and claiming possession. Rango is saying all the words I had wanted to hear you say. You never came close to me, even while taking me. You took me as men take foreign women in distant countries whose language they cannot speak. You took me in silence and strangeness. . . .)

When Rango fell asleep, when the aphrodisiac lantern had burnt out its oil, Djuna still lay awake, shaken by the echoes of his violence, and by the discovery that Rango's confidence would have to be reconstructed each day anew, that none of these maladies of the soul were curable by love or devotion, that the evil lay at the roots, and that those who threw themselves into palliating the obvious symptoms assumed an endless task, a task without hope of cure.

The word most often on his lips was *trouble*.

He broke the glass, he spilled the wine, he burnt the table with cigarettes, he drank the wine which dissolved his will, he talked away his plans, he tore his pockets, he lost his buttons, he broke his combs.

He would say: "I'll paint the door. I will bring oil for the lantern. I will repair the leak on the roof." And months passed: the door remained unpainted, the leak unrepaired, the lantern without oil.

He would say: "I would give my life for a few months of fulfillment, of achievement, of something I could be proud of."

And then he would drink a little more red wine, light another cigarette. His arms woud fall at his side; he would lie down beside her and make love to her.

When they entered a shop, she saw a padlock which they needed for the trap door and said: "Let's buy it."

"No," said Rango, "I have seen one cheaper elsewhere."

She desisted. And the next day she said: "I'm going near the place where you said they sold cheap padlocks. Tell me where it is and I'll get it."

"No," said Rango. "I'm going there today. I'll get it." Weeks passed, months passed, and their belongings kept disappearing because there was no padlock on the trap door.

No child was being created in the womb of their love, no child, but so many broken promises, each day an aborted wish, a lost object, a misplaced unread book, cluttering the room like an attic with discarded possessions.

Rango only wanted to kiss her wildly, to talk vehemently, to drink abundantly, and to sleep late in the mornings.

His body was in a fever always, his eyes ablaze, as if at dawn he were going to don a heavy steel armor and go on a crusade like the lover of the myths.

The crusade was the cafe.

Djuna wanted to laugh, and forget his words, but he did not allow her to laugh or to forget. He insisted that she retain this image of himself created in his talks at night, the image of his intentions and aspirations. Every day he handed her anew a spider web of fantasies, and he wanted her to make a sail of it and sail their barge to a port of greatness.

She was not allowed to laugh. When at times she was tempted to surrender this fantasy, to accept the Rango who created nothing, and said playfully: "When I first met you, you wanted to be a hobo. Let me be a hobo's wife," then Rango would frown severely and remind her of a more austere destiny, reproaching her for surrendering and dimishing his aims. He was unyielding in his desire that she should remind him of his promises to himself and to her.

This insistence on his dream of another Rango touched her compassion. She was deceived by his words and his ideal of himself. He had appointed her not only guardian angel, but a reminder of his ideals.

She would have liked at times to descend with him into more humanly accessible regions, into a carefree world. She envied him his reckless hours at the cafe, his joyous friendships, his former life with the gypsies, his careless adventures. The night he and his bar companions stole a rowboat and rowed up the Seine singing, looking for suicides to rescue. His awakenings sometimes in far-off benches in unknown quarters of the city. His long conversations with strangers at dawn far from Paris, in some truck which had given him a ride. But she was not allowed into this world with him.

Her presence had awakened in him a man suddenly whipped by his earlier ideals, whose lost manhood wanted to assert itself in action. With his conquest of Djuna he felt he had recaptured his early self before his disintegration, since he had recaptured his first ideal of woman, the one he had not attained the first time, the one he had completely relinquished in his marriage to Zora— Zora, the very opposite of what he had first dreamed.

What a long detour he had taken by his choice of Zora, who had led him into nomadism, into chaos and destruction.

But in this new love lay the possibility of a new world, the world he had first intended to reach and had missed, had failed to reach with Zora.

Sometimes he would say: "Is it possible that a year ago I was just a bohemian?"

She had unwittingly touched the springs of his true nature: his pride, his need of leadership, his early ambition to play an important role in history.

There were times when Djuna felt, not that his past life had corrupted him—because in spite of his anarchy, his destructiveness, the core of him had remained human and pure—but that perhaps the springs in him had been broken by the tumultuous course of his life, the springs of his will.

How much could love accomplish: it might extract from his body the poisons of failure and bitterness, of betrayals and humiliations, but could it repair a broken spring, broken by years and years of dissolution and surrenders?

Love for the uncorrupted, the intact, the basic goodness of another, could give a softness to the air, a caressing sway to the trees, a joyousness to the fountains, could

banish sadness, could produce all the symptoms of re-
birth. . . .

He was like nature, good, wild, and sometimes cruel.
He had all the moods of nature: beauty, timidity, violence,
and tenderness.

Nature was chaos.

"Way up into the mountains," Rango would begin
again, as if he were continuing to tell her stories of the
past which he loved, never of the past of which he was
ashamed, "on a mountain twice as high as Mont Blanc,
there is a small lake inside of a bower of black volcanic
rocks polished like black marble, in the middle of eternal
snow peaks. The Indians went up to visit it, to see the mirages. What I saw in the lake was a tropical scene, richly
tropical, palms and fruits and flowers. You are that to me,
an oasis. You drug me and at the same time you give me
strength."

(The drug of love was no escape, for in its coils lie latent
dreams of greatness which awaken when men and women
fecundate each other deeply. Something is always born of
man and woman lying together and exchanging the essences of their lives. Some seed is always carried and
opened in the soil of passion. The fumes of desire are the
womb of man's birth and often in the drunkenness of

caresses history is made, and science, and philosophy. For a woman, as she sews, cooks, embraces, covers, warms, also dreams that the man taking her will be more than a man, will be the mythological figure of her dreams, the hero, the discoverer, the builder. . . . Unless she is the anonymous whore, no man enters woman with impunity, for where the seed of man and woman mingle, within the drops of blood exchanged, the changes that take place are the same as those of great flowing rivers of inheritance, which carry traits of character from father to son to grandson, traits of character as well as physical traits. Memories of experience are transmitted by the same cells which repeated the design of a nose, a hand, the tone of a voice, the color of an eye. These great flowing rivers of inheritance transmitted traits and carried dreams from port to port until fulfillment, and gave birth to selves never born before. . . . No man and woman know what will be born in the darkness of their intermingling; so much besides children, so many invisible births, exchanges of soul and character, blossoming of unknown selves, liberation of hidden treasures, buried fantasies. . . .)

There was this difference between them: that when these thoughts floated up to the surface of Djuna's consciousness, she could not communicate them to Rango. He laughed at her. "Mystic nonsense," he said.

As Rango chopped wood, lighted the fire, fetched water from the fountain one day with energy and ebullience, smiling a smile of absolute faith and pleasure, then Djuna felt: wonderful things will be born.

But the next day he sat in the cafe and laughed like a rogue, and when Djuna passed she was confronted with another Rango, a Rango who stood at the bar with the bravado of the drunk, laughing with his head thrown back and his eyes closed, forgetting her, forgetting Zora, forgetting politics and history, forgetting rent, marketing, obligations, appointments, friends, doctors, medicines, pleasures, the city, his past, his future, his present self, in a temporary amnesia, which left him the next day depressed, inert, poisoned with his own angers at himself, angry with the world, angry with the sky, the barge, the books, angry with everything.

And the third day another Rango, turbulent, erratic, dark, like Heathcliff, said Djuna, destroying everything. That was the day that followed the bouts of drinking: a quarrel with Zora, a fight with the watchman. Sometimes he came back with his face hurt by a brawl at the cafe. His hands shook. His eyes glazed, with a yellow tinge. Djuna would turn her face away from his breath, but his warm, his deep voice would bring her face back saying: "I'm in trouble, bad trouble. . . ."

On windy nights the shutters beat against the walls like the bony wings of a giant albatross.

The wall against which the bed lay was wildly licked by the small river waves and they could hear the lap lap lap against the mildewed flanks.

In the darkness of the barge, with the wood beams groaning, the rain falling in the room through the unrepaired roof, the steps sounded louder and more ominous. The river seemed reckless and angry.

Against the smoke and brume of their caresses, these brusque changes of mood, when the barge ceased to be the cell of a mysterious new life, an enchanted refuge; when it became the site of compressed angers, like a load of dynamite boxes awaiting explosion.

For Rango's angers and battles with the world turned to poison. The world was to blame for everything. The world was to blame for Zora having been born very poor, of an insane mother, of a father who ran away. The world was to blame for her undernourishment, her ill health, her precocious marriage, her troubles. The doctors were to blame for her not getting well. The public was to blame for not understanding her dances. The house owner should have let them off without paying rent. The grocer had no right to claim his due. They were poor and had a right to mercy.

The noise of the chain tying and untying the rowboat, the fury of the winter Seine, the suicides from the bridge, the old watchman banging his pails together as he leaped over the gangplank and down the stairs, the water seeping too fast into the hold of the barge not pumped, the dampness gathering and painting shoes and clothes with mildew. Holes in the floor, unrepaired, through which the water gleamed like the eyes of the river, and through which the legs of the chairs kept falling like an animal's leg caught in a trap.

Rango said: "My mother told me once: how can you hope to play the piano, you have the hands of a savage."

"No," said Djuna, "your hands are just like you. Three of the fingers are strong and savage, but these last two, the smallest, are sensitive and delicate. Your hand is just like you; the core is tender within a dark and violent nature. When you trust, you are tender and delicate, but when you doubt, you are dangerous and destructive."

"I always took the side of the rebel. Once I was appointed chief of police in my home town, and sent with a posse to capture a bandit who had been terrorizing the

Indian villages. When I got there I made friends with the bandit and we played cards and drank all night."

"What killed your faith in love, Rango? You were never betrayed."

"I don't accept your having loved anyone before you knew me."

Djuna was silent, thinking that jealousy of the past was unfounded, thinking that the deepest possessions and caresses were stored away in the attics of the heart but had no power to revive and enter the present lighted rooms. They lay wrapped in twilight and dust, and if an old association caused an old sensation to revive it was but for an instant, like an echo, intermittent and transitory. Life carries away, dims, and mutes the most indelible experiences down the River Styx of vanished worlds. The body has its cores and its peripheries and such a mysterious way of maintaining intruders on the outer rim. A million cells protect the core of a deep love from ghostly invasions, from any recurrences of past loves.

An intense, a vivid present was the best exorcist of the past.

So that whenever Rango began his inquisitorial searchings into her memory, hoping to find an intruder, to battle Paul, Djuna laughed: "But your jealousy is necrophilic! You're opening tombs!"

"But what a love you have for the dead! I'm sure you visit them every day with flowers."

"Today I have not been to the cemetery, Rango!"

"When you are here I know you are mine. But when you go up those little stairs, out of the barge, walking in your quick quick way, you enter another world, and you are no longer mine."

"But you, too, Rango, when you climb those stairs, you enter another world, and you are no longer mine. You belong to Zora then, to your friends, to the cafe, to politics."

(Why is he so quick to cry treachery? No two caresses ever resemble each other. Every lover holds a new body until he fills it with his essence, and no two essences are the same, and no flavor is ever repeated. . . .)

"I love your ears, Djuna. They are small and delicate. All my life I dreamed of ears like yours."

"And looking for ears you found me!"

He laughed with all of himself, his eyes closing like a cat's, both lids meeting. His laughter made his high cheekbone even fuller, and he looked at times like a very noble lion.

"I want to become someone in the world. We're living on top of a volcano. You may need my strength. I want to be able to take care of you."

"Rango, I understand your life. You have a great force

in you, but there is something impeding you, blocking you. What is it? This great explosive force in you, it is all wasted. You pretend to be indifferent, nonchalant, reckless, but I feel you care deep down. Sometimes you look like Peter the Great, when he was building a city on a swamp, rescuing the weak, charging in battle. Why do you drown the dynamite in you in wine? Why are you so afraid to create? Why do you put so many obstacles in your own way? You drown your strength, you waste it. You should be constructing. . . ."

She kissed him, seeking and searching to understand him, to kiss the secret Rango so that it would rise to the surface, become visible and accessible.

And then he revealed the secret of his behavior to her in words which made her heart contract: "It's useless, Djuna. Zora and I are victims of fatality. Everything I've tried has failed. I have bad luck. Everyone has harmed me, from my family on, friends, everyone. Everything has become twisted, and useless."

"But Rango, I don't believe in fatality. There is an inner pattern of character which you can discover and you can alter. It's only the romantic who believes we are victims of a destiny. And you always talk against the romantic."

Rango shook his head vehemently, impatiently. "You

can't tamper with nature. One just is. Nature cannot be controlled. One is born with a certain character and if that is one's fate, as you say, well, there is nothing to be done. Character cannot be changed."

He had those instinctive illuminations, flashes of intuition, but they were intermittent, like lightning in a stormy sky, and then in between he would go blind again.

The goodness which at times shone so brilliantly in him was a goodness without insight, too; he was not even aware of the changes from goodness to anger, and could not conjure any understanding against his violent outbursts.

Djuna feared those changes. His face at times beautiful, human, and near, at others twisted, cruel, and bitter. She wanted to know what caused the changes, to avert the havoc they caused, but he eluded all efforts at understanding.

She wished she had never told him anything about her past. She remembered what incited her to talk. It was during the early part of the relationship, when one night he had leaned over and whispered: "You are an angel. I can't believe you can be taken like a woman." And he had hesitated for an instant to embrace her.

She had rushed to disprove it, eagerly denying it. She had as great a fear of being told that she was an angel as other women had of their demon being exposed. She felt it was not true, that she had a demon in her as everyone had, but that she controlled it rigidly, never allowing it to cause harm.

She also had a fear that this image of the angel would eclipse the woman in her who wanted an earthy bond. An angel to her was the least desirable of bedfellows!

To talk about her past had been her way to say: "I am a woman, not an angel."

"A sensual angel," then he conceded. But what he registered was her obedience to her impulses, her capacity for love, her gift of herself, on which to base henceforth his doubts of her fidelity.

"And you're Vesuvius," she said laughing. "Whenever I talk about understanding, mastering, changing, you get as angry as an earthquake. You have no faith that destiny can be changed."

"The Mayan Indian is not a mystic, he is a pantheist. The earth is his mother. He has only one word for both mother and earth. When an Indian died they put real food in his tomb, and they kept feeding him."

"A symbolical food does not taste as good as real food!"

(It is because he is of the earth that he is jealous and possessive. His angers are of the earth. His massive body is of the earth. His knees are of iron, so strong from pressing against the flanks of wild horses. His body has all the flavors of the earth: spices, ginger, chutney, musk, pimiento, wine, opium. He has the smooth neck of a statue, a Spanish arrogance of the head, an Indian submission, too. He has the awkward grace of an animal. His hands and feet are more like paws. When he catches a fleeing cat he is swifter than the cat. He squats like an Indian and then leaps on powerful legs. I love the way his high cheekbones swell with laughter. Asleep he shows the luxuriant charcoal eyelashes of a woman. The nose so round and jovial; everything powerful and sensual except his mouth. His mouth is small and timid.)

What Djuna believed was that like a volcano his fire and strength would erupt and bring freedom, to him and to her. She believed the fire in him would burn all the chains which bound him. But fire too must have direction. His fire was blind. But she was not blind. She would help him.

In spite of his physical vitality, he was helpless, he was bound and tangled. He could set fire to a room and destroy, but he could not build as yet. He was bound and blind as nature is. His hands could break what he held out of strength, a strength he could not measure, but he could not build. His inner chaos was the chain around his body, his conviction that one was born a slave of one's nature, to be led inevitably to destruction by one's blind impulses.

"What do you want your life to be?"

"A revolution every day."

"Why, Rango?"

"I love violence. I want to serve ideas with my body."

"Men die every day for ideas which betray them, for leaders who betray them, for false ideals."

"But love betrays, too," said Rango. "I have no faith."

(Oh, god, thought Djuna, will I have the strength to win this battle against destruction, this private battle for a human love?)

"I need independence," said Rango, "as a wild horse needs it. I can't harness myself to anything. I can't accept any discipline. Discipline discourages me."

Even asleep his body was restless, heavy, feverish. He threw off all the blankets, lay naked, and by morning the bed seemed like a battlefield. So many combats he had waged within his dreams; so tumultuous a life even in sleep.

Chaos all around him, his clothes always torn, his books soiled, his papers lost. His personal belongings, of which he remembered an object now and then which he missed, wanted to show Djuna, were scattered all over the world, in rooming-house cellars where they were kept as hostages for unpaid rent.

All the little flames burning in him at once, except the wise one of the holy ghost.

It saddened Djuna that Rango was so eager to go to war, to fight for his ideas, to die for them. It seemed to her that he was ready to live and die for emotional errors as women did, but that like most men he did not call them emotional errors; he called them history, philosophy, metaphysics, science. Her feminine self was sad and smiled, too, at this game of endowing personal and emotional beliefs with the dignity of impersonal names. She smiled at this as men smile at women's enlargement of personal tragedies to a status men do not believe applicable to personal lives.

While Rango took the side of wars and revolutions, she took the side of Rango, she took the side of love.

Parties changed every day, philosophies and science changed, but for Djuna human love alone continued.

Great changes in the maps of the world, but none in this need of human love, this tragedy of human love swinging between illusion and human life, sometimes breaking at the dangerous passageway between illusion and human life, sometimes breaking altogether. But love itself as continuous as life.

She smiled at man's great need to build cities when it was so much harder to build relationships, his need to conquer countries when it was so much harder to conquer one heart, to satisfy a child, to create a perfect human life. Man's need to invent, to circumnavigate space when it is so much harder to overcome space between human beings, man's need to organize systems of philosophy when it was so much harder to understand one human being, and when the greatest depths of human character lay but half explored.

"I must go to war," he said. "I must act. I must serve a cause."

Rango gave her the feeling of one who reproduced in life gestures and scenes and atmosphere already imprinted on her memory. Where had she already seen Rango on horseback, wearing white fur boots, furs and corduroys, Rango with his burning eyes, somber face, and wild black hair?

Where had she already seen Rango's face in passion worshipful like a man receiving communion, the profane wafer on the tongue?

Seeing him lying at her side was like one of those memories which assail one while traveling through foreign lands to which one was not bound in any conscious way, and yet at each step recognizing its familiarity, with an exact prescience of the scene awaiting one around the corner of the street.

Memory, or race memories, or the influence of tales, fairy tales, legends, and ballads heard in childhood?

Rango came from sixteenth-century Spain, the Spain of the troubadours, with its severity, its rigid form, the domination of the church, the claustration of women, the splendor of Catholic ceremonies, and a vast, secret tumultuous river of sensuality running below the surface, uncontrollable, and detectable only through those persistent displays of guilt and atonement common to all races.

Rango recreated for Djuna a natural blood-and-flesh paradise so different from the artificial paradises created in art by city children. In her childhood spent in cities, and not in forests, she had created paradises of her own inventions, with a language of her own, outside and beyond life, as certain birds create a nest in some inaccessible branch of a tree, inaccessible to disaster but also difficult to preserve.

But Rango's paradise was an artless paradise of life in a forest, in mountains, lakes, mirages, with strange animals and strange flowers and trees, all of it warm and accessible.

Because she had been a child of the cities, the paradise of her childhood had been born of fairy tales, legends, and mythology, obscuring ugliness, cramped rooms, miserly backyards.

Rango had had no need to invent. He had possessed mountains of legendary magnificence, lakes of fantastic proportions, extraordinary animals, a house of great beauty. He had known fiestas which lasted for a week, carnivals, orgies. He had taken his ecstasies from the rarefied air of heights, his drugs from religious ceremonies, his physical pleasures from battles, his poetry from solitude, his music from Indian dances, and been nourished on tales told by his Indian nurse.

To visit the first girl he had loved he had had to travel all night on horseback, he had leaped walls, and risked

75

her mother's fury and possible death at the hands of her father. It was all written in the *Romancero!*

The paradise of her childhood was under a library table covered to the ground by a red cloth with fringes, which was her house, in which she read forbidden books from her father's vast library. She had been given a little piece of oilcloth on which she wiped her feet ostentatiously before entering this tent, this Eskimo hut, this African mud house, this realm of the myth.

The paradise of her childhood had been in books.

The house in which she had lived as a child was the house of the spirit which does not live blindly but is ever, out of passionate experience, building and adorning its four-chambered heart—an extension and expansion of the body, with many delicate affinities establishing themselves between her and the doors and passageways, the lights and shadows of her outward abode, until she was incorporated into it in the entire expressiveness of what is outward as related to the inner significance, until there was no more distinction between outward and inward at all.

(I'm fighting a dark force in Rango, loving nature in him, through him, and yet fighting the destructions of nature. When my life culminates in a heaven of passion, it is most dangerously balanced over a precipice. The further I seek to soar into the dream, the essence, touching the vaults of the sky, the tighter does the cord of reality press my neck. Will I break seeking to rescue Rango? Fatigue of the heart and body. . . . Intermittently I see and feel the dampness, poverty, a sick Zora, food on the table with wine stains, cigarette ashes, and bread crumbs of past meals. Only now and then do I notice the rust in the stove, the leak in the roof, the rain on the rug, the fire that has gone out, the sour wine in a cup. And thus I descend through trap doors without falling into a trap but knowing there is another Rango I cannot see, the one who lives with Zora, who awaits to appear in the proper lighting. And I am afraid, afraid of pain. . . . Now I understand why I loved Paul . . . because he was afraid. When we lay down and caressed each other we caressed this self-same fear and understood it, under the blanket, fear of violence. We recognized it in the dark, with our hands and our mouths. We touched it and were moved by it, because it was our secret which we shared through the body. Everyone says: you must take sides, choose a political party, choose a philosophy, choose a dogma. . . . I chose the dream of human love. Whatever I ally myself to is to be close to my love. With it I hope to defeat tragedy, to defeat violence. I dance, I sew, I mend, I cook for the sake of this dream. In this dream nobody dies, nobody is sick, nobody separates. I love and dance with my dream unfurled, trusting darkness, trusting the labyrinth, into the furnaces of love. Some say: the dream is escape. Some say: the dream is madness. Some say: the dream is sickness. It will betray you. The Rango I see is not the one Zora sees, or the world sees. This is the witchcraft of love. You can take sides in religion, you can take sides in history, and there are others with you, you are not alone. But when you take the side of love, the opium of love, you are alone. For the doctors call the dream a symptom, the historians escape, the philosophers a drug, and even your lover will not make the perilous journey with you. . . . Hang your dream of love on the mast of this barge of caresses . . . a flag of fire. . . .)

The enemy was not outside as Rango believed.

What he most wanted to avoid, which was that Djuna should remember her days with Paul, or desire Paul's return, or yearn for his presence, was the very feeling he caused by his violence. Because his violence drove her away from him. The sense of devastation left by his angry words, or his distorted interpretations of her acts, his doubts, caused such an anxious climate that at times to escape from the tension, like a child seeking peace and gentleness, she did remember Paul. . . .

Then Rango committed a second error: he wanted Djuna and Zora to be friends.

Djuna never knew whether he believed this would achieve a unity in his torn and divided life, whether he was thinking only of himself, or of sharing his burden with Djuna, or whether he had such faith in Djuna's creation of human beings that he hoped she could heal Zora and perhaps win Zora's affection and put an end to the tension he felt whenever he returned home.

The obscurities and labyrinths of Rango's mind remained always mysterious to her. There were twists and deformities in his nature which she could not clarify. Not only because he never knew himself what took place within him, not only because he was full of contradictions and confusions, but because he resented and rebelled against any examination, probing, or questioning of his motives.

So came the day when he said: "I wish you would visit Zora. She is very ill and you might help her."

Until now there had been very little mention of Zora. Certain words of Rango's had accumulated in Djuna's mind: Rango had married Zora when he was seventeen. Six years before he met Djuna they had begun to live together without a physical bond, "as brother and sister." She was constantly ill and Rango had a great compassion

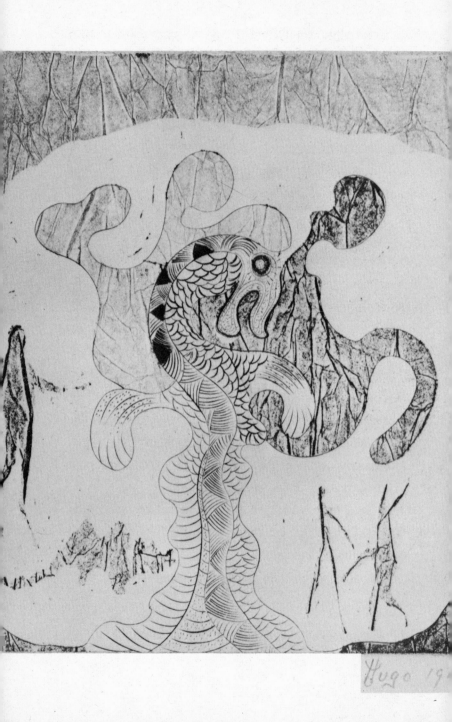

for her helplessness. Djuna did not know whether more than compassion bound them together, more than the past.

She knew that this appeal was made to her good self, and that she must, to answer it, subdue her own wishes not to be entangled in Rango's life with Zora, or to avoid a relationship which could only cause her pain. She was being asked to bring a certain aspect of herself among her other aspects as others are asked to wear a certain costume out of their multiple wardrobe.

She was invited to bring her good self only, in which Rango believed utterly, and yet she felt a rebellion against this good self which was too often called upon, was too often invited, to the detriment of other selves who were now like numerous wallflowers! The Djuna who wanted to laugh, to be carefree, to have a love all of her own, an integrated life, a rest from troubles.

Secretly she had often dreamed of her other selves, the wild, the free, the natural, the capricious, the whimsical, the mischievous ones. But the constant demand upon the good one was atrophying the others.

But there are invitations which are like commands.

There are heraldic worlds of spiritual and emotional aristocracy which have nothing to do with conventional morality, which give to certain acts a quality of noblesse oblige, a faithfulness to the highest capacities of a personality, a sort of life on the altitudes, a devotion to the idealized self. The artists who had overthrown conventions submitted to this code and knew the sadness and guilt which came from any failing in this voluntary standard. All of them suffered at times from a guilt resembling the guilt of the religious, the moralists, the bourgeois, while apparently living in opposition to them. It was the incurable guilt of the idealist seeking to reach an image of one's self one could be proud of.

They had merely created fraternities, duties, communal taboos of another sort, but to which they adhered at the cost of great personal sacrifices.

Djuna did not know how this good self had attained such prominence. She did not know how it had come to be born at all, for she considered it thrust upon her, not adopted by her. She felt much less good than she was expected to be. It gave her a feeling of treachery, of deception.

She did not have the courage to say: I would rather not see Zora, not know your other life. I would rather retain my illusion of a single love.

In childhood she remembered she played dangerous games. She sought adventures and difficulties. She fabricated paper wings and threw herself out of a second-story window, escaping injury by a miracle. She did not want to be the sweet and gentle heroine in charades and games, but the dark queen of intrigue. She preferred Catherine de' Medici to the flavorless and innocent princesses.

She was often tangled in her own high rebellions, in her devastating bad tempers, and in lies.

But her parents repeated obsessionally: You must be good. You must keep your dress clean. You must be kind, thank the lady, hide your pain if you fall, do not reach for anything you want, do not attract attention to yourself, do not be vain about the ribbon in your hair, efface yourself, be silent and modest, give up to your brothers the games they want, curb your temper, do not talk too much. all do not invent stories about things which never happened, *be good or else you will not be loved*. And when she was accused of any of these offenses, both parents turned away from her and she was denied the good-night or good-morning kiss which was essential to her happiness. Her mother carried out her threats of loss into games which seemed like tragedies to Djuna the child: once swimming in a lake before Djuna's anxious eyes, she had pretended to disappear and be drowned. When she reappeared on the surface Djuna was already hysterical. Another time, in a vast railroad station, when Djuna was six years old, the mother hid behind a column and Djuna found herself alone in the crowd, lost, and again she wept hysterically.

The good self was formed by these threats: an artificial bloom. In this incubator of fear, her goodness bloomed merely as the only known way to hold and attract love.

There were other selves which interested her more but which she learned to conceal or to stifle: her inventive fantasy weaving self who loved tales, her high-tempered self who flared like heat lightning, her stormy self, the lies which were not lies but an improvement on reality.

She had loved strong language like ginger upon the lips. But her parents had said: "From you we don't expect this, not from you." And appointed her as a guard upon her brothers, asking her to enforce their laws, just as Rango had appointed her now a guard against his disintegrations.

So that she had learned the only reconciliation she could find: she learned to preserve the balance between crime and punishment. She took her place against the wall, face to the wall, and then muttered, "Damn damn damn damn," as many times as she pleased, since she was simultaneously punishing herself and felt absolved, with no time wasted on contrition.

And now this good self could no longer be discarded. It

had a compulsive life, its legend, its devotees! Every time she yielded to its sway she increased her responsibilities, for new devotees appeared, demanding perpetual attendance.

If Rango asked her today to take care of Zora, it was because he had heard, and he knew, of many past instances when she had taken care of others.

This indestructible good self, this false and wearying good self who answered prayers: Djuna, I need you; Djuna, console me; Djuna, you carry palliatives (why had she studied the art of healing, all the philters against pain?); Djuna, bring your wand; Djuna, we'll take you to Rango, not the Rango of the joyous guitar and the warm songs, but Rango, the husband of a woman who is always ill. It will break your heart, Djuna of the fracturable heart, your heart will fracture with a sound of wind chimes and the pieces will be iridescent. Where they fall new plants will grow instantly and it is to the advantage of a new crop of breakable hearts that yours should fracture often, for the artist is like the religious man, he believes that denial of worldly possessions, pain, and trouble will bring not sainthood but art, will give birth to the marvelous.

(This goodness is a role, too tight around me; it is a costume I can no longer wear. There are other selves trying to be born, demanding at least a hearing!)

Your past history influenced your choice, Djuna; you have shown capabilities to lessen pain and so you are not invited to the fiestas.

Irrevocable extension of past roles, and no reversal possible.

Too many witnesses to past compassions, past abdications, and they will look scandalized by any alteration of your character and will reawaken your old guilts. Face to the wall! This time so that Rango may not see your rebellion in your face. Rango's wife is mortally ill and you are to bring your philters.

But she had made an important discovery.

This bond with Rango, this patience with his violent temper, this tacit fraternity of her gentleness and his roughness, this collaboration of light and shadow, this responsibility for Rango which she felt, her compulsion to rescue him from the consequences of his blind rages, were because Rango lived out for her this self she had buried in her childhood. All that she had denied and repressed: chaos, disorder, caprice, destruction.

The reason for her indulgence; everyone marveled (how could you bear his jealousy, his angers?) at the way he destroyed what she created so that each day she must begin anew: to understand, to order, to reconstruct, to mend; the reason for her acceptance of the troubles caused by his blindness was that Rango *was* nature, uncontrolled, and that the day she had buried her own laziness, her own jealousy, her own chaos, these atrophied selves awaited liberation and began to breathe through Rango's acts. For this complicity in the dark she must share the consequences with him.

The realm she had tried to skip: darkness, confusion, violence, destruction, erupted secretly through relationship with Rango. The burden was placed on his shoulder. She must therefore share the torments, too. She had not annihilated her natural self; it reasserted itself in Rango. And she was his accomplice.

The dark-faced Rango who opened the door of his studio below street level was not the joyous carefree guitarist Djuna had first seen at the party, nor was it the fervent Rango of the nights at the barge, nor was it the oscillating Rango of the cafe, the ironic raconteur, the reckless adventurer. It was another Rango she did not know.

In the dark hallway his body appeared silhouetted, his high forehead, the fall of his hair, his bow, full of nobility, grandeur. He bowed gravely in the narrow hallway as if this cavernous dwelling were his castle, he the seigneur and she a visitor of distinction. He emerged prouder, taller, more silent, too, out of poverty and barrenness, since they were of his own choice. If he had not been a rebel, he would be greeting her at the vast entrance of his ranch.

Down the stairs into darkness. Her hand touched the walls hesitantly to guide herself, but the walls had such a rough surface and seemed to be sticky to the touch so that she withdrew it and Rango explained: "We had a fire here once. I set fire to the apartment when I fell asleep while smoking. The landlord never repaired the damage as we haven't paid rent for six months."

A faint odor of dampness rose from the studio below, which was the familiar odor of poor studios in Paris. It was compounded of fog, of the ancient city breathing its fetid breath through cellar floors; it was the odor of stagnation, of clothes not often washed, of curtains gathering mildew.

She hesitated again until she saw the skylight windows above her head; but they were covered with soot and let in a dim northern light.

Rango then stood aside, and Djuna saw Zora lying in bed.

Her black hair was uncombed and straggled around her parchment-colored skin. She had no Indian blood, and her face was almost a direct contrast to Rango's. She had heavy, pronounced features, a wide full mouth, all cast in length, in sadness, a defeated pull downward which only changed when she raised her eyelids; then the eyes had in them an unexpected shrewdness which Rango did not have.

She was wearing one of Rango's shirts, and over that a kimono which had been dyed black. The red and black squares of the shirt's colors showed at the neck and wrists. The stripes once yellow still showed through the black dye of the kimono.

On her feet she wore a pair of Rango's big socks filled with cotton wool at the toes, which seemed like disproportionate clown's feet on her small body.

Her shoulders were slightly hunched, and she smiled the smile of the hunchback, of a cripple. The arching of her shoulders gave her an air of having shrunk herself together to occupy a small space. It was the arch of fear.

Even before her illness, Djuna felt, she could never have been handsome but had a strength of character which must have been arresting. Yet her hands were childish and clasped things without firmness. And in the mouth there was the same lack of control. Her voice, too, was childish.

The studio was now half in darkness, and the oil lamp which Rango brought cast long shadows.

The mist of dampness in the room seemed like the breath of the buried, making the walls weep, detaching the wallpaper in long wilted strips. The sweat of centuries of melancholic living, the dampness of roots and cemeteries, the moisture of agony and death seeping through the walls seemed appropriate to Zora's skin from which all glow and life had withdrawn.

Djuna was moved by Zora's smile and plaintive voice. Zora was saying: "The other day I went to church and prayed desperately that someone should save us, and now you are here. Rango is always bewildered, and does nothing." Then she turned to Rango: "Bring me my sewing box."

Rango brought her a tin cracker box which contained needles, threads, and buttons in boxes labeled with medicine names: Injections, drops, pills.

The material Zora took up to sew looked like a rag. Her small hands smoothed it down mechanically, yet the more she smoothed it down the more it wilted in her hands, as if her touch were too anxious, too compressing, as if she transmitted to objects some obnoxious withering breath from her sick flesh.

And when she began to sew she sewed with small stitches, closely overlapping, so closely that it was as if she were strangling the last breath of color and life in the rag, as if she were sewing it to the point of suffocation.

As they talked she completed the square she had already begun, and then Djuna watched her rip apart her labor and quietly begin again.

"Djuna, I don't know if Rango told you, but Rango and I are like brother and sister. Our physical life . . . was over years ago. It was never very important. I knew that sooner or later he would love another woman, and I am glad it's you because you're kind, and you will not take him away from me. I need him."

"I hope we can be . . . kind to each other, Zora. It's a difficult situation."

"Rango told me that you never tried, or even mentioned, his leaving me. How could I not like you? You saved my life. When you came I was about to die for lack of care and food. I don't love Rango as a man. To me he is a child. He has done me so much harm. He just likes to drink, and talk, and be with friends. If you love him, I am glad, because of the kind of woman you are, because you are full of quality."

"You're very generous, Zora."

Zora leaned over to whisper now: "Rango is mad, you know. He may not seem so to you because he is leaning on you. But if it were not for you I would be out in the street, homeless. We've often been homeless, and I'd be sitting on my valises, out on the sidewalk, and Rango just waving his arms and helpless, never knowing what to do. He lets everything terrible happen, and then he says: 'It's destiny.' With his cigarette he set fire to our apartment. He was nearly burnt to death."

There was a book lying at the foot of her bed, and Djuna opened it while Zora was carefully unstitching all she had sewed before.

"It's a book about illness," said Zora. "I love to read about illness. I go to the library and look up descriptions of the symptoms I have. I've marked all the pages which apply to me. Just look at all these markings. Sometimes I think I have all the sicknesses one can have!" She laughed. Then looking at Djuna plaintively, almost pleadingly, she said: "All my hair is falling out."

When Djuna left that evening, Rango and she were no longer man and woman in a chamber of isolated love for each other. They were suddenly a trinity, with Zora's inexorable needs conducting all their movements, directing their time together, dictating the hours of separation.

Rango had placed Zora under Djuna's protection and her love for Rango had to extend in magnitude to include Zora.

Zora talked to Djuna. If it was Djuna who had planned to come to Zora and show the most exemplary devotion, she found herself merely passive before the friendliness of Zora.

It was Zora who talked, with her eyes upon her sewing and unsewing. "Rango is a changed man, and I'm so happy, Djuna. He is kinder to me. He was very unhappy before and he took it out on me. A man cannot live without love and Rango was not easy to satisfy. All the women wanted him, but he would see them once perhaps and come back dejected, and refuse to see them again. He always found something wrong with them. With you he is content. And I am happy because I knew this had to happen sometime, but I'm happy it's you because I trust you. I used to fear some woman coming and taking him where I would never see him again. And I know you wouldn't do that."

Djuna thought: "I love Rango so much that I want to share his burdens, love and serve what he loves and serves, share his conviction that Zora is an innocent victim of life, worthy of all sacrifices."

This was for both Rango and Djuna the atonement for the marvelous hours in the barge. All great flights away from life land one in such places of atonement as this room, with Zora sewing rags and talking about dandruff, about ovarian insufficiency, about gastritis, about thyroid and neuritis.

Djuna had brought her a colorful Indian-print dress and Zora had dyed it black. And now she was reshaping it and it looked worn and dismal already. She wore a shawl pinned with a brooch which had once held stones in its clasps and was now empty, thrusting bare silver branches out like the very symbol of denudation. She wore two overcoats sewn together, the inner one showing at the edges.

While they sat sewing together, Zora lamented over Rango: "Why must he always live with so many people around him?"

Knowing that Rango liked to spend hours and hours

alone with her, Djuna feared to say: "Perhaps he is just seeking warmth and forgetfulness, running away from illness and darkness."

When Rango was with her he seemed dominating, full of dignity and pride. When he entered Zora's room he seemed to shrink. When he first entered there was a copper glow in his face; after a moment the glow vanished.

"Why do men live in shoals?" persisted Zora.

Djuna looked at Rango lighting the fire, warming water, starting to cook. There was something so discouraged in the pose of his body, expressing agreement with Zora's enumeration of his faults, so diminished, which Djuna could not bear to witness.

Zora was in the hospital.

Djuna was cooking for Rango now, and also a special soup which Rango was to take to Zora at noon.

As Djuna passed through the various rooms to find Zora she saw a woman sitting up in bed combing her hair and tying a blue ribbon around it. Her face was utterly wasted, and yet she had powdered it, and rouged her lips, and there was on it not only the smile of a woman dying but also the smile of a woman who wanted to die with grace, deploying her last flare of feminine coquetry for her interview with death.

Djuna was moved by this courage, the courage to meet death with one's hair combed, and this gentle smile issuing from centuries of conviction that a woman must be pleasing to all eyes, even to the eyes of death.

When she reached Zora's bed she was faced with the very opposite, an utter absence of courage, although Zora was less ill than the other woman.

"The soup is not thin enough," said Zora. "It should have been strained longer." And she laid it aside and shook her head while Djuna and Rango pleaded that she should eat it anyway for the sake of gaining strength.

Her refusal to eat caused Rango anxiety, and Zora watched this anxiety on his face and savoured it.

He had brought her a special bread, but it was not the one she wanted.

Djuna had brought her some liver concentrate in glass containers. Zora looked at them and said: "They are not good. They're too dark. I'm sure they're not fresh and they will poison me."

"But Zora, the date is printed on the box, the drugstore can't sell them when they're old."

"They're very old, I can see it. Rango, I want you to get me some others at La Muette drugstore."

La Muette was one hour away. Rango left on his errand and Djuna took the medicine away.

When they met in the evening Rango said: "Give me the liver medicine. I'll take it back to the drugstore."

They walked to the drugstore together. The druggist was incensed and pointed to the recent date on the box.

What amazed Djuna was not that Zora should give way to a sick woman's whims, but that Rango should be so utterly convinced of their rationality.

The druggist would not take it back.

Rango was angry and tumultuous, but Djuna was rebelling against Rango's blindness and when they returned to the houseboat she opened one of the containers and before Rango's eyes she swallowed it.

"What are you doing?" asked Rango with amazement.

"Showing you that the medicine is fresh."

"You believe the druggist and not Zora?" he said angrily.

"And you believe in a sick person's whim," she said.

Zora was always talking about her future death. She began all her conversations with: "When I die. . . ." Rango was maintained in a state of panic, fearing her death, and lived each day accordingly: "Zora is in grave danger of death," he would say, to excuse her demands upon his time.

At first Djuna was alarmed by Zora's behavior, and shared Rango's anxieties. Her gestures were so vehement, so magnified, that Djuna believed they might be those of a dying woman. But as these gestures repeated themselves day after day, week after week, month after month, year after year, Djuna lost her fear of Zora's death.

When Zora said: "I have a burning sensation in my stomach," she made the gestures of a person writhing in a brasier of flames.

At the hospital, where Djuna sometimes accompanied her, the nurses and doctors no longer listened to her. Djuna caught glances of irony in the doctor's eyes.

Zora's gestures to describe her troubles became for Djuna a special theatre of exaggeration, which at first caused terror, and then numbed the senses.

It was like the Grand Guignol, where knowing every scene was overacted to create horror finally created detachment and laughter.

But what helped Djuna to overcome her terror was

something else which happened that winter: there was an epidemic of throat infection which swept Paris and which Djuna caught.

It was painful but came without fever, and there was no need to stay in bed.

That same day Rango rushed to the barge, distressed and vehement. He could not stay with Djuna because Zora was terribly ill. "You might come back with me, if you wish. Zora has a heart attack, an inflamed throat, and she's suffocating."

When they arrived, the doctor was there examining Zora's throat. Zora lay back pale and rigid, as if her last hour had come. Her gestures, her hands upon her throat, her strained face were a representation of strangulation.

The doctor straightened up and said: "Just the same throat infection everybody has just now. You don't have to stay in bed. Just keep warm, and eat soups only."

And Djuna, with the same throat trouble, was out with Rango.

The first year Djuna had suffered from Rango's panic. The second year from pity; the third year detachment and wisdom came. But Rango's anxiety never diminished.

Djuna awakened one morning and asked herself: "Do I love this woman who magnifies her illness a thousand times, unconcerned with curing it, but savoring its effect on others? Why does Zora contort herself in a more than life-size pain for all the world to see and hear?"

Many times Djuna had been baffled by the fact that when someone said to Zora, "You look better, so much better," Zora was not pleased. A frown would come between her eyes, an expression of distress.

At the hospital one day, the doctor did not linger very long at Zora's bedside, and when he walked away Djuna laid her hand on his arm: "Please tell me what's the matter with my friend?"

"She's a pathological case," he said.

Djuna saw the second face of Zora.

It was an expression she had seen before and could not place. And then she remembered.

It was the expression upon the face of professional beggars. Her enumeration of the troubles she had endured that day was like the plaintive incantation too perfectly molded by time and repetition.

Under the tone of sorrow there was a practice in the tone of sorrow.

Yet Djuna felt ashamed to doubt the sincerity of Zora's complaints, as one is ashamed to doubt a beggar's poverty. Yet she felt, as one does occasionally before a beggar, that a pain too often studied for public exposure had become a pain necessary to the beggar, his means of livelihood, his claim to existence, to protection. If he were deprived of it, he would be deprived of his right to compassion.

It was as if true compassion should be reserved for troubles not exploited, but of recent occurrence and deeply felt. The poverty of the professional lamenter was an asset rather than a tragedy.

Djuna wanted to forget her intuition, in favor of the tradition which dictated that a beggar's needs cannot be judged, because there is a noblesse oblige which dictates: his cup is empty and yours is full, therefore there is only one action possible; and even if an investigation revealed the beggar not to be blind and to have amassed a fortune under his pallet, even then, such hesitations before an empty cup are so distressing that the role of the believer is easier, easier to be deceived than to doubt. . . .

Djuna was sometimes disconcerted by the shrewd look

in Zora's eyes while she detailed her day's hardships; as startled to catch this expression as to see a blind man who was crossing the street alone and walking into danger—causing you a sharp compassion—to see him suddenly turn upon you eyes fully aware of the impending danger.

But Djuna wanted to believe, because Rango believed. She discarded this first glimpse of Zora's second face as people often discard first intuitions until they reach the end of a friendship, the end of a love, and then this long-buried first impression reappears only to prove that the animal senses in human beings warning them clearly of dangers, of traps, may be accurate but are often discarded in favor of a blind compulsion in the opposite direction to that of self-preservation. Proving that human beings have a sense of danger but that some other desire, some other compulsion, lures and draws them precisely toward these traps, toward self-destruction.

Djuna felt now like a puppet. She felt the need to give Rango a perpetually healthy, perpetually spirited woman because at home he had a perpetually sick, depressed wife. Rango's needs set the tone, mood, and activities of her days. She obeyed the strings blindly. She allowed Rango's anxieties to infect her, merely so he would not be alone with his burden. The strings were in Zora's hands. The hierarchy was firmly established: if Zora had a cold, a headache, Rango must stay at home (even if this cold were caused by Zora washing her hair in the middle of a winter day and going out with her hair still wet). It was forbidden to rebel or question the origin of the trouble, or to suggest that Zora might consider others, consider preventing these troubles.

Zora could not cook, could not shop, could not clean, she could not be alone at night. If friends came to see her, Rango must be at home to save her pride.

When Djuna had first known Rango he spent most of his nights out at the cafe. Often he did not come home till dawn, and oftener still he did not come home at all when he was spending a night with one of his mistresses.

At first Zora had said: "I'm so glad to know Rango is not drinking, that he is with you instead of at the cafe."

But after a while she developed new fears. Rango said: "Poor Zora, she is so afraid at night. The other evening someone knocked at her door for a long time and just stood there waiting. She was so frightened that the man would come in and rape her that she piled all the furniture in front of the door and did not sleep all night."

Rango spent every other night at the barge, and then only twice a week as Zora's complaints increased, and then one night a week.

And on that one night Zora came and knocked on the door.

She was in pain, she said. Rango rushed out and took her home. She was convulsed with pains. The doctor was called, and could not find the cause. Only at dawn did she confess: she had heard that cleaning fluid was good for the stomach, so she had drunk a glass of it.

Rango left Djuna to watch over Zora while he went to buy the medicines which the doctor advised.

Djuna tended Zora, and Zora smiled at her innocently. Could Zora be so unaware of the consequences of her acts?

Whenever they were alone together they fell naturally into a sincere relationship. Djuna's compassion would once more be aroused and Zora would nestle into it securely. At these moments Djuna believed a relationship was being constructed to which Zora would be loyal, one of mutual giving. It was only later that Djuna would discover what Zora had achieved with her behavior, and that would always be, in the end, something to harm and stifle the relationship between Rango and Djuna.

But it was all so subtly done that Djuna could never detect it.

When Zora talked about Rango, it seemed at first a natural harmless sick woman's complaining; it seemed not as if she wanted to harm Rango in Djuna's eyes, but as if she wanted Djuna's sympathy for her difficult life with Rango. It was only later when alone that Djuna became aware of how much dissension and doubt Zora had managed to insert in her monotonous lamentations against Rango.

Djuna would prepare herself for these talks which hurt her by thinking: "She is talking about another Rango, not the one I know. The Rango I love is different. This is the Rango that was born of his life with Zora. She is responsible for what he was with her."

This night, calmed by Djuna's ministrations, Zora began to talk: "You love Rango in such a different way than I do. I never loved Rango physically. I never loved any man physically. I don't know what it is to respond to a man. . . . You know, sometimes when I get these crying spells, I think to myself: maybe it's because I can't melt physically. I don't feel anything, and so crying is a relief, I cry instead. . . ."

Djuna was moved by this, and then appalled. Rango did not know about Zora's coldness. Was this the secret of her destructiveness toward him?

She wished she did not have to become an intimate part of their lives together. She wished she could escape the clutch of Zora's dependence.

She was silent. Zora was beginning her usual long, monotonous recital of Rango's faults: It was Rango who had made her ill. It was Rango who had ruined her career. Rango was to blame for everything.

Zora blamed Rango, and Rango blamed the world. Both of them were equally blind in the knowledge of their own character and responsibilities. Djuna did not know yet, but sensed the cause of their downfall.

Djuna rebelled against Rango's blind subservience to Zora's helplessness, and yet she found herself in the same position: unable to avoid the slavery.

Zora never asked a favor. She demanded, and then proceeded to criticize how the orders were carried out, with a sense of her right to be served and no acknowledgment or lightest form of thankfulness.

Zora was now talking about her career as a dancer: "I was the first to present Guatemalan dances to Paris audiences. I was very successful, so much so that an agent came from New York and arranged a tour for me. I made money, I made many friends. But there was a woman in the show traveling with me who wanted to kill me."

"Oh, no, Zora."

"Yes, for no reason at all. She invited me to lunch with her every day and gave me tomatoes and eggs. They made me terribly ill. They were poisoned."

"Perhaps they weren't poisoned; perhaps eggs and tomatoes don't agree with you."

"She did it on purpose, I tell you, I was too much of a success."

(That's madness, thought Djuna. If only Rango would realize this, we could live in peace. If he would detach himself and admit: she is very ill, she is unbalanced. We could take care of her but not let her destroy our life together. But Rango sees everything as distortedly as she does. If only he would *see*. It would save us all.)

"Zora, what I can't understand was why, if you were so successful as a dancer, if you reached the heights there, and could travel, and do all you wanted . . . what happened? What caused the downfall in your life? Was it your health?"

Zora hesitated. Djuna was painfully tense, awaiting an answer to this question, feeling that if Zora answered it their three lives would be altered.

But Zora never answered direct questions.

Djuna regretted having used the word downfall. Downfall was the wrong word for Zora and Rango, since all their troubles were caused by an evil world, came from a hostile aggression from the world.

Zora sank into apathy. Would she deviate as Rango

did, elude, answer so elliptically that the question would be lost in a maze of useless vagaries.

She reopened her eyes and began her recitation where she had left off: "In New York I stopped the show. The agent came to see me with a long contract. I could make as much money as I wanted to. I had fur coats and beautiful evening dresses, I could travel. . . ."

"And then?"

"Then I left everything and went home to Guatemala."

"Home to Guatemala?"

Zora laughed, irrepressibly, hysterically, for such a long time that Djuna was frightened. A spasm of cough stopped her. "You should have seen the face of the agent, when I didn't sign the contract. Everybody's face. I enjoyed that. I enjoyed their faces more than I enjoyed the money. I left them all just like that and went home. I wanted to see Guatemala again. I laughed all the way, thinking of their faces when I quit."

"Were you sick then?"

"I was always sick, from childhood. But it wasn't that. I'm independent."

Djuna remembered Rango telling her the story of a friend who had worked to obtain an engagement for Zora in Paris, a contract to dance at a private house. He had promised to meet this friend at the cafe. "I came five hours late, and she was in a state." Whenever he told this story he laughed. The idea of this friend waiting, foaming and furious, sitting at the cafe, aroused his humor.

"I stayed six months in Guatemala. When my money was gone I returned to New York. But nobody would sign me up. They told each other about the broken contract. . . ."

Rango arrived with the medicine. Zora refused to take it. Bismuth would calm her pain and the burn, but she refused to take it. She turned her face to the wall and fell asleep, holding Djuna and Rango's hand, both enchained to her caprices.

Djuna's head was bowed. Rango said: "You must be exhausted. You'd better go home. Sometimes I think. . . ." Djuna raised imploring eyes to his face, wildly hoping that they would be united by the common knowledge that Zora was a sick, unstable child who needed care but who could not be allowed to direct, to infect their lives with her destructiveness.

Rango looked at her, his eyes not seeing what she saw. "Sometimes I think you're right about Zora. She does foolish things. . . ." And that was all.

He walked to the door with her. . . . She looked into the bleak and empty street. It was just before dawn. She needed warmth, sleep. She needed to be as blind as Rango was, to continue living this way. The knowledge she had was useless. It only added to her burden, the knowing that so much effort, care, devotion were being utterly wasted, that Zora would never be well, that it was wrong to devote two lives to one twisted human being. . . . This knowledge estranged her from Rango, whose blind faith she could not share. It burdened her, isolated her. Tonight, through fatigue, she wanted so much to lay her head on Rango's shoulder, to fall asleep in his arms, but there was already another head on his shoulder, a heavy burden.

As if in fear that Djuna should ask him to come with her, he said: "She cannot be left alone."

Djuna was silent. She could not divulge what she knew.

When she did protest against the excessive demands and whims of Zora, even gently, Rango would say: "I am between two fires, so you must help me."

To help him meant to yield to Zora, knowing that she would in the end destroy their relationship.

Every day Djuna suppressed her knowledge, her lucidity; Rango would have considered them an attack upon a defenseless Zora.

Noblesse oblige enforced silence, and all her awareness of the destruction being wrecked upon their relationship —when Zora was the greatest beneficiary of this relationship—only served to increase her suffering.

Zora had mysteriously won all the battles; Rango and Djuna could never spend a whole night together.

What corrodes a love are the secrets.

This doubt of Zora's sanity which she dared not word to Rango, which made every sacrifice futile, created a fissure in the closeness to Rango. A simple, detached understanding of this would have made Rango less enslaved, less anxious, and would have brought Djuna and Rango closer together, whereas his loyalty to all the irrational demands of Zora, her distorted interpretation of his acts as well as Djuna's, was a constant irritant to Djuna's intelligence and awareness.

The silence with which she accomplished her duties now became a gradual isolation in her emotions.

It was strange to be cooking, to be running errands, to be searching for new doctors, to be buying clothes, to be furnishing a new room for Zora, while knowing that Zora was working against them all and would never get well because her illness was her best treasure, was her weapon of power over them.

But Rango needed desperately to believe. He believed that every new medicine, every new doctor would restore her health.

Djuna felt now as she had as a child, when she had repudiated her religious dogmas but must continue to attend mass, rituals, kneel in prayer, to please her mother.

Any departure from what he believed he considered a betrayal of her love.

At every turn Zora defeated this battle for health. When she got a new room in the sun, she kept the blinds down and shut out air and light. When they went to the beach together up the river, her bathing suit, given to her by Djuna, was not ready. She had ripped it apart to improve its shape. When they went to the park she wore too light a dress and caught cold. When they went to a restaurant she ate the food she knew would harm her, and predicted that the next day she would be in bed all day.

She made pale attempts to take up her dancing again, but never when alone, only when Djuna and Rango were there to witness her pathetic attempts, and when the exertion would cause her heart to beat faster she would say to Rango: "Put your hand here. See how badly my heart goes when I try to work again."

At times Djuna's detachment, her self-protective numbness would be annihilated by Rango, as when he said once: "We are killing her."

"We are killing her?" echoed Djuna, bewildered and shocked.

"Yes, she said once that it was my unfaithfulness which made her ill."

"But unfaithful to what, Rango? She was not your wife, she was your sick child, long before I came. It was understood between you that your relationship was fraternal, that sooner or later you would need a woman's love. . . ."

"Zora didn't mind when I had just a desire for a woman, a passing desire. . . . But I gave you more than that. That's what Zora cannot accept."

"But Rango, she told me that she was happy and secure with our relationship, because she felt protected by both of us, she knew I would not take you away from her, she said she had gained two loves and lost nothing. . . ."

"One can say such things, and yet feel betrayed, feel hurt. . . ."

Rango convinced Djuna that their love must be atoned for. Even if Zora had always been ill, even as a child, even though their love protected her, yet they must atone . . . atone . . . atone. Never enough devotion could make up for what pain they caused her. . . . Not enough to rise early in the morning to market for tempting foods for

113

Zora, never enough to dress her, to answer her every whim, to surrender Rango over and over again.

Djuna fell into an overwhelming, blind, stupefying devotion to Zora. She became the sleeping dreamer seeking nothing but one brief moment of fiery joy with Rango, and then atoning for it the rest of the time.

Rango would ring her bell and call her out during the night to watch Zora while he went for medicines.

The sleeping dreamer Djuna walked up a muddy hill on a rainy afternoon to the hospital bringing Zora her winter coat, so divested and stripped of her possessions that her father was beginning to notice it and demanded explanations: "Where is your coat? Why aren't you wearing stockings? You're beginning to dress like a tramp recently. Is this the influence of your new friends? Who are you associating with?"

Rango's grateful kisses over her eyelids were the blinding, drugging hypnosis, and she let her father believe that she was "fancying herself a bohemian now," that she was playing at being poor.

That afternoon at the hospital Rango left her alone with Zora. The moment he left the room Zora said: "Reach for that bottle on the shelf. It's a disinfectant. Pour some here in the bassinet. The nurse is stingy with it. She measures only a few drops. She doesn't want me to get well. She's saving the stuff. And I know more of it would cure me."

"But Zora, this stuff is strong. It will burn your skin. You can't use a lot of it. The nurse isn't trying to economize."

An expression of utter maliciousness came into Zora's eyes: "You want me to die, don't you? So you can live with Rango. That's why you won't give me the medicine."

Djuna gave her the bottle and watched Zora pouring the strong liquid in the bassinet. She would burn her skin, but she would at least believe that Djuna was on her side.

Rango's long oriental eyes which opened and closed like a cat's, his oblique dark eyes, would soon close hers upon reality, upon all reasoning.

He did not observe the coincidences as Djuna did unconsciously. Whenever Djuna went away for a few days Zora would be moderately ill. Whenever Djuna returned there would be an aggravation, and thus Djuna and Rango could not meet that evening.

Djuna instinctively knew this to be so accurate and inevitable that she would prepare herself for it. On her way back from a trip she would say to herself: "Don't get exalted at the idea of seeing Rango, for surely Zora will get very ill when you come back and Rango will not be free. . . ."

115

And then because Rango could not explode or revolt against an illness (which he thought genuine and inevitable), could not see how its developments obeyed Zora's destructive will, he revolted at other situations, unjustly, inaccurately. Djuna learned to detect the origin of the revolt, to know it was an aborted revolt at home which he diverted and brought to other scenes or circumstances. He exploded wildly over politics, he attacked the illnesses of other women, he incited other husbands to revolt and would seek them out and take them to the cafe almost by force, just as Djuna indulged now and then in a tirade against helpless or childish women in general because she did not dare to speak openly against Zora's childishness.

From so many scenes at home Rango escaped to Djuna as a refuge. He would place the whole weight of his head and arms on her knees, and if it happened that Djuna was tired, she did not reveal it for fear of overburdening a man too heavily burdened already. She disguised her own needs, her weaknesses, her handicaps, her own fears or troubles. She concealed them all from him. Thus grew in his mind an image of her infinite energy, infinite power to overcome obstacles. Any flaw in this irritated him like a failed promise. He needed her strength.

Because he seemed to love Zora for her weakness, to be so indulgent toward her inadequacies, her fumbling inability to open a door, incapacity to buy a stamp and mail a letter, to visit a friend alone, Djuna felt a deep unbalance, a deep injustice taking place. For the extreme childishness of Zora robbed her relation to Rango of all its naturalness. It set the two women at opposite poles, not as rivals, but as opposites, destruction against construction, weakness against strength, taking against giving.

To break the hypnosis came certain shocks, which Djuna was losing her power to interpret.

When she had gradually passed to Zora most of her belongings, all of her jewelry—to such an extreme that she had to surrender going to certain places and seeing certain friends where she could not appear dressed as carelessly as she was—she arrived unexpectedly at Zora's and found her sitting among six opened trunks.

"I'm working on a costume for a new dance," said Zora.

The trunks overflowed with clothes. Not theatre costumes only, but coats, dresses, stockings, underwear, shoes.

Djuna looked bewildered and Zora began to show her all that the trunks contained, explaining: "I bought all this when things were going well for me in New York."

"But you could wear them now!"

"Yes, I could, but they look too nice. I just like to keep them and look at them now and then."

And all the time she had been wearing torn shoes, mended stockings, dresses too light for winter, when not wearing all that she had extracted from Djuna.

This discovery stunned Djuna. It proved what she had felt all the time obscurely, that Zora's dramatization of the poor, the cold, the scantily dressed, the pathetic woman, was a voluntary role which suited her deepest convenience. That this drabness, which constantly aroused Rango's pity, was deliberate, that, at any moment, she could have been better dressed than Djuna.

That night Djuna could not refrain from asking Rango: "Did you know when I gave up my fur coat for Zora to wear this winter, that she had one in her trunk all the time?"

"Yes," said Rango. "Zora has a lot of the gypsy in her. Gypsies always keep their finery for certain occasions, and like to look at it now and then, but seldom wear it."

"Am I going mad?" asked Djuna of herself. "Or is Rango as mad as Zora? He is not aware of the absurdity, the cruelty of this. He thinks it's natural that I should dispossess myself for a woman obsessed with the desire to arouse pity."

119

But as this incident threatened her faith in Rango, she soon closed her eyes again.

The actor does not suffer any cramps because he knows the role he plays he will be able to discard at some stated time, and walk free again to be himself.

But Djuna's role in life seemed inescapable. She was doomed to be devoted to a cause she did not believe in. Zora would never get well; Rango would never be free. She suffered from pains which were like cramps, because in all these unnatural positions she took, these contortions of giving, of surrender, there was a strain from the knowledge that she could never, as long as she loved Rango, ever be free and herself again.

Out of physical exhaustion she would occasionally run away.

This time to conceal her exhaustion from Rango she took the Dover-Calais boat intending to hide in London for a few days at the house of a friend.

Sitting on deck, on a foggy afternoon, she felt so utterly tired and discouraged that she fell asleep. Tired tired tired, her body sank into deep sleep on the deck chair. Sleep. A deep deep sleep . . . until she felt a hand on her shoulder as if calling. She would not open her eyes; she would not respond. She dreaded to awaken. She feigned a complete sleep and turned her head away from the hand that was beckoning . . .

But the voice persisted: "Mademoiselle, mademoiselle. . . ."

A voice pleading.

She felt the spray on her face, the swaying of the ship, and began to hear the voices around her.

She opened her eyes.

A man was leaning over her, his hand still on her shoulder.

"Mademoiselle, forgive me. I know I should have let you sleep. Forgive me."

"Why did you wake me? I was so tired, so tired." She was not fully awake yet, not awake enough to be angry, or even reproachful.

"Forgive me. I can explain, if you will let me. I am not trying to flirt, believe me. I'm a *grand blessé de guerre.* I can't tell you how seriously wounded, but it's left me so I can't bear fog, damp, rain, or the sea. Pains. Such pains all over the body. I have to make this trip often, for my work. It's torture, you know. Going back to England now. . . . When the pains start there is nothing I can do but to talk to someone. I had to talk to someone. I looked all around me. I looked into every face. I saw you asleep. I know it was inconsiderate, but I felt: that's the woman I can talk to. It will help me—do you mind?"

"I don't mind," said Djuna.

And they talked, all the way, on the train, too, all the way to London. When she reached London she was near collapse. She took the first hotel room she could find and slept for twelve hours. Then she returned to Paris.

No more questioning, no more interpretations, no more examinations of her life. She was resigned to her destiny. It was her destiny. The *grand blessé de guerre* on the ship had made her feel it, had convinced her.

So she made a pirouette charged with sadness, on the revolving stages of awareness, and returned to this role she had been fashioned for, even down to the face, even when asleep.

But when people play a role motivated by false impulses, moved by compulsions formed by fear, by distortions, rather than by a deep need, the only symptom which reveals that it is a role and that acts do not correspond to the true nature, is the sense of unbearable tension.

The ways to measure one's insincerities are few, but Djuna knew that the most infallible one was joylessness. Any task accomplished without joy was a falsity to one's true nature. When Djuna indulged in an extravagant giving to Zora she felt no joy because it was misinterpreted by both Rango and Zora. If there was a natural goodness in Djuna it was not this magnified, this self-destructive annihilation of all of herself.

But this role could last a lifetime, since Rango denied the possibility of change by clairvoyance, the possibility of a lucid change of direction. They were rudderless and at the mercy of Zora's madness.

She did not even gain the prestige granted to the professional actor, for there is this about roles played in life, and that is that no one is deceived. The most obtuse, the most insensitive people feel a dissonance, sense an imposture, and, whereas the actor is respected for creating an illusion on the stage, no one is respected for seeking to create an illusion in life.

She planned another escape, this time with Rango and Zora. She felt that taking them to the sea, into nature, might heal them all, might strengthen Zora and bring them peace.

It was a most arduous undertaking to get Zora to pack

and to free Rango from all his tangles. They missed not one but several trains. Zora had two trunks of belongings. Rango had debts and his debtors were reluctant to let him leave Paris. They overslept in the mornings.

Rango borrowed some money and bought Djuna a present, a slender white-leather belt from Morocco. It was his first present and Djuna was overjoyed and wore it proudly. But when the three met at the station she found Zora wearing an identical belt, so her own lost its charm for her and she threw it away.

The fishing port they reached in the morning lay in the sun. The crescent-shaped harbor sheltered yachts and fishing boats from all over the world. The cafes were all gathered on the edge and as they sat having coffee they saw the boats come to life, the sailors and voyagers emerging from their cabins. They saw the small portholes open, the hatches lifted, and sails spread. They saw the sailors starting to polish brass and wash decks.

Behind them rose the hills planted with white houses built during the Moor's invasion of the Mediterranean coast.

The place was animated, like a perpetual carnival. The fluttering, glitter, and mobility of the harbor and ships were reflected in the cafes and visitors. Women's scarfs answered the coquetries of the sails. The eyes, skins, and smiles were as polished as the brass. Women's sea-shell necklaces reflected the sky and the sea.

Rango found a place for Zora and himself at the top of a hill within a forest. Djuna took a room in a hotel farther down the hill and nearer to the harbor.

When Rango came down the hill on his bicycle and met Djuna at one of the cafes on the port, the sun was setting.

The night and the sea were velvety and caressing, unfolding a core of softness. As the plants exhaled a more mysterious flowering, people, too, shed their brighter day selves and donned colors and perfumes more appropriate to secret blooms. They dilated with the leaves, the shadows, at the approach of night.

The automobiles which passed carried all the flags of pleasure unfurled in audacious smiles, insolent scarfs.

All the voices were pitched to a tone of intimacy. Sea, earth, and bodies seeking alliances, wearing their plumage of adventure, coral and turquoise, indigo and orange. Human corollas opening in the night, inviting pursuit, seeking capture, in all the dilations which allow the sap to rise and flow.

Then Rango said: "I must leave. Zora is afraid of the dark."

To make it easier for Rango she bicycled back with him, but when she returned alone to her room all the exhalations of the sea tempted her out again, and she returned to the port and sat at the same table where she had sat with Rango and watched the gaiety of the port as she had watched that first party out of her window as a girl, feeling again that all pleasure was unattainable for her.

People were dancing in the square to an accordion played by the village postmaster. The letter carrier invited her to dance, but all the time she felt Rango's jealous and reproachful eyes on her. Every porthole, every light, seemed to be watching her dance with reproach.

So at ten o'clock she left the port and its festivities and bicycled back to her small hotel room.

As she climbed the last turn in the hill, pushing her bicycle before her, she saw a flashlight darting over her window which gave on the ground floor. She could not see who was wielding it, but she felt it was Rango and she called out to him joyously, thinking that perhaps Zora had fallen asleep and he was free and had come to be with her.

But Rango responded angrily to her greeting: "Where have you been?"

"Oh, Rango, you're too unjust. I couldn't stay in my room at eight o'clock. It's only ten now, and I'm back early, and alone. How can you be angry?"

But he was.

"You're too unjust," she said, and passing by him, almost running, she went into her room and locked the door.

The few times that she had held out against him, such as the time he had arrived at midnight instead of for dinner as he had promised, she had noticed that Rango's anger abated, and that his knock on the door had not been imperious, but gentle and timid.

That is what happened now. And his timidity disarmed her anger.

She opened the door. And Rango stayed with her and they sought closeness again, as if to resolder all that his violence broke.

"You're like Heathcliff, Rango, and one day everything will break."

He had an incurable jealousy of her friends, because to him friends were the accomplices in the life she led outside of his precincts. They were the possible rivals, the witnesses, and perhaps the instigators to unfaithfulness. They were the ones secretly conniving to separate them.

But graver still was his jealousy of the friends who reflected an aspect of Djuna not included in her relationship to Rango, or which revealed aspects of Djuna not encompassed in the love, an unknown Djuna which she

127

could not give to Rango. And this was a playful, a light, a peace-loving Djuna, the one who delighted in harmony, not in violence, the one who found outside of passion luminous moods and regions unknown to Rango. Or still the Djuna who believed understanding could be reached by effort, by an examination of one's behavior, and that destiny could be reshaped, one's twisted course redirected with lucidity.

She attracted those who knew how to escape the realm of sorrow by fantasy. Other extensions of Paul appeared, and one in particular of whom Rango was as jealous as if he had been a reincarnation of Paul. Though he knew it was an innocent friendship, still he stormed around it. He knew the boy could give Djuna a climate which his violence and intensity destroyed.

It was her old quest for a paradise again, a region outside of sorrow.

Lying on the sand with Paul the second (while Rango and Zora slept through half of the day) they built ninepins out of driftwood, they dug labyrinths into the sand, they swam under water looking for sea plants, and drugged themselves with tales.

Their only expression of a bond was his reaching for her little finger with his, as Paul had once done, and this was like an echo of her relation to Paul, a fragile bond, a bond like a game, but life-giving through its very airiness and delicacy.

Iridescent, ephemeral hours of relief from darkness.

When Rango came, blurred, soiled by his stagnant life with Zora, from quarrels, she felt stronger to meet this undertow of bitterness.

She wore a dress of brilliant colors, indigo and saffron; she brushed her hair until it glistened, and proclaimed in all her gestures a joyousness which she hoped would infect Rango.

But as often happened, this very joyousness alarmed him; he suspected the cause of it, and he set about to reclaim her from a region she had not traversed with him, the region of peace, faith, and gentleness he could never give her.

True that Paul the second had only appropriated her little finger and laid no other claim on her, true that Rango's weight upon her body was like the earth, stronger and warmer, true that when his arms fell at her side with discouragement they were so heavy that she could not have lifted them, true that those made only of earth and fire were never illuminated, never lifted or borne above it, never free of it, but hopelessly entangled in its veins.

Her dream of freeing Rango disintegrated day by day. When she gave them the sun and the sea, they slept. Zora had ripped her bathing suit and was sewing it again. She would sew it for years.

It was clear to Djuna now that the four-chambered heart was no act of betrayal, but that there were regions necessary to life to which Rango had no access. It was not that Djuna wanted to house the image of Paul in one chamber and Rango in another, nor that to love Rango she must destroy the chamber inhabited by Paul—it was that in Djuna there was a hunger for a haven which Rango was utterly incapable of giving to her, or attaining with her.

If she sought in Paul's brother a moment of relief, a moment of forgetfulness, she also sought in the dark, at night, someone without flaw, who would protect her and forgive all things.

Whoever was without flaw, whoever understood, whoever contained an inexhaustible flow of love was god the father whom she had lost in her childhood.

Alone at night, after the torments of her life with Rango, after her revolts against this torment which she had vainly tried to master with understanding of Rango, defeated by Rango's own love of this inferno, because he said it was real, it was life, it was heightened life, and that happiness was a mediocre ideal, held in contempt by the poets, the romantics, the artists—alone at night when she acknowledged to herself that Rango was doomed and would never be whole again, that he was corrupted in his love of pain, in his belief that war and troubles heightened the flavor of life, that scenes were necessary to the climax of desire, like fire, suddenly in touching the bottom of the abysmal loneliness in which both relationships left her, she felt the presence of god again, as she had felt him as a child, or still at another time when she had been close to death.

She felt this god again, whoever he was, taking her tenderly, holding her, putting her to sleep. She felt protected, her nerves unknotted, she felt peace. She fell asleep, all her anxieties dissolved. How she needed him, whoever he was, how she needed sleep, she needed peace, she needed god the father.

In the orange light of the fishing port, the indigo spread of the sea, the high flavor of the morning rolls, the joyousness of early mornings on the wharf, the scenes with Rango became more and more like hallucinations.

Rango walking through the reeds seemed like a Balinese, with his dark skin and blazing eyes.

When they sat at the beach late at night around a fire and roasted meat, he seemed so in harmony with nature, crouching on his strong legs, nimble with his hands. When they returned from long bicycle rides, after hours of pedaling against a brisk wind, tired and thirsty but drugged with physical euphoria and content, then the returns to his obsessions seemed more like a sickness.

Djuna knew all the prefaces to trouble. If during the ride she had sung in rhythm with others, or laughed, or acquiesced, Rango would begin: "This morning I found your bicycle and the boy's against the wall of the cafe, so close together, as if you had spent the night together."

"But Rango, he arrived after me, he merely placed his bicycle next to mine. Everyone has breakfast at the same cafe. It doesn't mean anything."

At times Djuna felt that Rango had caught Zora's madness. Then she felt compassion for him, and would answer with patience, as you would a sick person.

She knew that we love in others some repressed self.

In consoling Rango, reassuring him, was she consoling some secret Djuna who had once been jealous and not dared to reveal it?

(We love shadows of our hidden selves in others. Once I must have been as jealous as Rango, but I did not reveal it, even to myself. I must have experienced such jealousy in so hidden a realm of my own nature that I was not even aware of it. Or else I would not be so patient with Rango. I would not feel compassion. He is destroying us both by this jealousy. I want to protect him from the consequences . . . He is driving me away from him. I should run away now, yet I feel responsible. When we see another daring to be what we did not dare, we feel responsible for him. . . .)

But once she awakened so exhausted by Rango's demon that she decided to frighten him, to run away, hoping it might cure him.

She packed and went to the station. But there was no train until evening. She sat disconsolately to wait.

And Rango arrived. He looked distracted. "Djuna! Djuna, forgive me. I must have been mad. I didn't tell you the truth. A friend of mine has been making absinthe in his cellar and every day at noon we have been sampling it. I must have taken a good deal of it all these days."

She forgave him. She also thought, in an effort always

to absolve him: "His slavery to Zora's needs is so tremendous and he does not dare to rebel. She has a gift for making him feel that he never does enough, and to burden him with guilt, and that may be why, when he comes to me, he has to rebel and be angry about something, he has to explode. I am his scapegoat."

And she was tied to Rango through this breathing tube, tied to his explosions. She might one day come to believe, as he did, that violence was necessary to dive to the depths of experience.

On these revolving stages of the unconscious, the last hidden jungles of our nature which we have controlled and harnessed almost to extermination, sealing all the wells, it is no wonder when we seek to open these sealed wells again to find a flow of life we find instead a flow of anger.

Thus in anger Rango threw like a geyser this nature's poison, and then refused to admit responsibility for the storms. His angers came like lightning, and each time Djuna was delivered of her own.

But the black sun of his jealousy eclipsed the Mediterranean sun, churned the sea's turquoise gentleness.

There were times when she lay alone on the sand and sought to remember what she had tried to reach through the body of Rango, what her first sight of him, playing on his guitar and evoking his gypsy life, had awakened in her.

Through him, to extend into pure nature.

There were times when she remembered his first smile, the ironic smile of the Indian which came from afar like the echo of an ancient Indian smile at the beginning of Mayan worlds; the earthy walk issued from bare footsteps treading paths into the highest mountains of the world, into the most immune lakes and impenetrable forests.

In her dream of him she returned to the origins of the world, hearing footsteps in Rango which were echoes of primeval footsteps hunting.

She remembered, above all, stories, the one Rango had told her about sitting on a rock on top of a glacier and asserting he had felt the spinning of the earth!

She had kissed eyes filled with remembrance of splendors, eyes which had seen the Mayans bury their gold treasures at the bottom of the lakes out of reach of the plundering Spaniards.

She had kissed the Indian princes of her childhood fairytales.

She had plunged with love and desire into the depths of ancient races, and sought heights and depths and magnificence.

And found . . . found deserts where vultures perpetuated their encirclement, no longer distinguishing between the living and the dead.

Found a muted city resting on ruined columns, cracked cupolas, tombs, with owls screaming like women in childbirth.

In the shadows of volcanoes there were fiestas, orgies, dances, and guitars.

But Rango had not taken her there.

To love he brought only his fierce anxieties; she had embraced, kissed, possessed a mirage. She had walked and walked, not into the fiestas and the music, not into laughter, but into the heart of an Indian volcano. . . .

The trap was visible by day.

The trap was a web of senseless duties. No sooner were Djuna's eyes open than she saw Zora vividly, lying down, pale, with soft flabby hands touching everything with infantile awkwardness. Zora missing her aim, dropping what she held, fumbling with a door, and moving so abnormally slowly and with such hazy, uncertain gestures that it took her two hours to get dressed.

Compassion was the cover with which Djuna disguised to her own eyes her revulsion for Zora's whining voice, unkempt body, and shrewd glance, for her beggar's clothes which were a costume to attract pity, for the listless hair she was too lazy to brush, for the dead skin through which the blood stagnated.

If one knew what lay in Zora's mind, one would turn away with revulsion. Djuna had heard her sometimes, half asleep, monotonously accusing doctors, the world, Rango, herself, friends, for all that befell her.

Revulsion. There is a guilt not only for acts committed but for one's thoughts. Now that the trap had grown so grotesque, futile, stifling, Djuna wished every day that Zora might die. A useless life, grasping food, devotion, service, and giving absolutely nothing, less than nothing. A useless life, exuding poison, envy, a strangling tyranny.

If she died, Rango's life might soar again, a fire, his body strong and exuberant, his imagination propelling him to all corners of the world. At his worst moments, there was always a fire in him. In Zora there was coldness. Only the mind at work, deforming, denigrating, accusing.

Only a showman left in her. "See my wound, see what I suffer. Love me."

But love is not given for such reasons.

The trap is inescapable. Djuna has nightmares of Zora's yellow face and lack of courage. She awakens early, to market for a special bread, a special meat, a special vegetable. There is an appointment for x-rays of the chest, for this week Zora believes she has tuberculosis. Hours wasted on this, only to hear the doctor say: "There's nothing wrong. Hysterical symptoms. She should be taken to a psychiatrist."

There is a visit to the pawnbroker, because one must pay the other doctor, the one who made the futile, the dramatic, test for cancer. Djuna's allowance for the month is finished.

There is no escape. The day crumbles soon after it is born. The only tree she will see will be the anemic tree of the hospital garden.

A useless, abortive sacrifice gives sadness.

The day is the trap, but she does not dare revolt. If she wants her half-night with Rango, this is the only path to reach it. At the end of the day there will be his fervent kisses, his emotion, his desire, the bites of hunger on the shoulder, vibrations of pleasure shaking the body, the guttural moans of men and women returning to their primitive origin. . . .

Sometimes there is no time for undressing. At others,

the climax is postponed teasingly, arousing frenzy. The dross of the day is burned away.

When Djuna thinks during the day, "I must run away. I must leave Rango to his chosen torment," it is the remembrance of this point of fire which binds her.

How can Rango admire Zora's rotting away—not even a noble suicide, but a fixed obsession to die slowly, dragging others along with her? A life ugly and monstrous. If she washes a dish, she complains. It she sews a button, she laments.

These are Djuna's thoughts, and she must atone for them, too. Zora, take this bread I traveled an hour to find, it won't nourish you, you are too full of poison within your body. Your first words to me were hypocritical, your talk about praying to be helped, and being glad I was the one, yes, because I was one who could be easily caught through compassion. You knew I would act toward you as you would never have acted toward me. I have tried to imagine you in my place, and I couldn't. I know you would be utterly cruel.

On her way back to the barge she bought new candles, and a fur rug to lie on, because Rango believed it was too bourgeois to sleep on a bed like everybody else. They slept on the floor. Perhaps a fur, the bed of Eskimos, would be appropriate.

When Rango came, he looked at the candles and the fur like a lion looking at a lettuce leaf. But lying on it, his bronze desire is aroused and the primitive bed is baptized in memory of cavernous dwellings.

At this hour children are reading fairy tales from which Rango and Djuna were led to expect such marvels, the impossible. Rango had imagined a life without work, without responsibilities. Djuna had wanted a life of desire and freedom, not comfort but the smoothness of magical happenings, not luxury but beauty, not security but fulfillment, not perfection but a perfect moment like this one . . . but without Zora waiting to lie between them like an incubus. . . .

Djuna was unprepared for Rango's making the first leap out of the trap. It came unexpectedly at midnight as they were about to separate. Out of the fog of enswathing caresses came his voice: "We're leading a selfish life. There are many things happening in the world; we should be working for them. You are like all the artists, with your big floodlights fixed on the sky, and never on earth, where things are happening. There is a revolution going on, and I want to help."

Djuna did not think of the world or the revolution needing Rango, Rango and his bohemian indiscipline, his love of red wine, his laziness. She felt that Zora's persecutions were driving him away. He was caught between a woman who wanted to die, and one who wanted to live! He had hoped to amalgamate the women, so he would not feel the tension between his two selves. He had thought only of his own emotional comfort. He had overlooked Zora's egoistic ferocity, and Djuna's clairvoyance. The alliance was a failure.

Now he was driven to risk his life for some impersonal task.

She was silent. She looked at his face and saw that his mouth looked unhappy, wounded, and revealed his desperateness. He kept it tightly shut, as women do when they don't want to weep. His mouth which was not in keeping with his lion's head, which was the mouth of a child, small and vulnerable; the mouth which aroused her indulgence.

Parting at the corner of the street, they kissed desperately as if for a long voyage. A beggar started to play on his violin, then stopped, thinking they were lovers who would never see each other again.

The blood beat in her ears as she walked away, her body parting from Rango in anticipation, hair parting from hair, hands unlocking, lips closing against the last kiss, surrendering him to a more demanding mistress: the revolution.

The earth was turning fast. Women cannot walk out of the traps of love, but men can; they have wars and revolutions to attend to. What would happen now? She knew. One signed five sheets of papers and answered minute, excruciatingly exact questions. She had seen the questionnaire. One had to say whether one's wife or husband believed in the revolution; one had to tell everything. Rango would be filling these pages slowly, with his nervous, rolling, and swaying handwriting. Everything. He would probably say that his wife was a cripple, but the party would not condone a mistress.

Then suddenly the earth ceased turning and the blood no longer rang in her ear. Everything stood deathly still because she remembered the dangers. . . . She remembered Rango's friend who had been found with a bullet hole in his temple, near the cafe where they met. She remembered Rango's story about one of the men who worked for the revolution in Guatemala: the one who had been placed in a jail half full of water until his legs rotted away in strips of moldy flesh, until his eyes turned absolutely white.

The next evening Rango was late. Djuna forgot that he was always late. She thought: he has signed all the papers, and been told that a member of the party cannot have a mistress.

It was nine o'clock. She had not eaten. It was raining. Friends came into the cafe, talked a little, and left. The time seemed long because of the anxiety. This is the way it would be, the waiting, and never knowing if Rango were still alive. He would be so easily detected. A foreigner, dark skin, wild hair, his very appearance was the one policemen expected from a man working for the revolution.

What had happened to Rango? She picked up a newspaper. Once he had said: "I picked up a newspaper and saw on the front page the photograph of my best friend, murdered the night before."

That is the way it would happen. Rango would kiss her as he had kissed her the night before at the street corner, with the violin playing, then the violin would stop, and that very night. . . .

She questioned her instinct. No, Rango was not dead.

She would like to go to church, but that was forbidden, too. Despair was forbidden. This was the time for stoicism.

She was jealous of Rango's admiration for Gauguin's mother, a South American heroine, who had fought in revolutions and shot her own husband when he betrayed the party.

Djuna walked past the church and entered. She could

not pray because she was seeking to transform herself into the proper mate for a revolutionist. But she always felt a humorous, a private, connivance with god. She felt he would always smile with irony upon her most wayward acts. He would see the contradictions, and be indulgent. There was a pact between them, even if she were considered guilty before most tribunals. It was like her friendliness with the policemen of Paris.

And now Rango walked toward her! (See what a pact she had with god that he granted her wishes no one else would have dared to expect him to grant!)

Rango had been ill. No, he had not signed the papers. He had overslept. Tomorrow. *Mañana.*

Djuna had forgotten this Latin deity: *Mañana.*

At the Cafe Martiniquaise, near the barge, Rango and Djuna sat drinking coffee.

The place was dense with smoke, voices, faces, heaving and swaying like a compact sonorous wave, washing over them at times and enswathing them, at others retreating as if subdued, only to return again louder and more suffocating to engulf their voices.

Djuna could never identify such a tide of faces dissolved by lights and shadows, slightly blurred in outlines from drink. But Rango could say immediately: "There's a pimp, there's a prizefighter. There's a drug addict."

Two friends of Rango's walked in, with their hands in their pockets, greeted them obliquely, with heavy lids half dropped over glazed eyes. They had deep purple shadows under the eyes and Rango said: "It startles me to see my friends disintegrating so fast, even dying, from drugs. I'm no longer drawn to this kind of life."

"You were drawn toward destruction before, weren't you?"

"Yes," said Rango, "but not really. When I was a young man, at home, what I liked most was health, physical energy and well-being. It was only later, here in Paris the poets taught me not to value life, that it was more romantic to be desperate, more noble to rebel, and to die, than to accept what ordinary life had to offer. I'm not drawn to that any more. I want to live. That was not the real me. Zora says you changed me, yet I can't think of anything you said or did to accomplish it. But every time we are together I want to accomplish something, something big. I don't want any more of this literary credo, about the romantic beauty of living desperately, dangerously, destructively."

Djuna thought with irony that she had not meant to give birth to a rebel. She had changed, too, because of Rango. She had acquired some of his gypsy ways, some of his nonchalance, his bohemian indiscipline. She had swung with him into the disorders of strewn clothes, spilled cigarette ashes, slipping into bed all dressed, falling asleep thus, indolence, timelessness. . . . A region of chaos and moonlight. She liked it there. It was the atmosphere of earth's womb, where awareness could not reach and illumine all the tragic aspects of unfulfilled desires. In the darkness, chaos, warmth, one forgot. . . . And the silence. She liked the silence most of all. The silence in which the body, the senses, the instincts, are more alert, more powerful, more sensitized, live a more richly perfumed and intoxicating life, instead of transmuting into thoughts, words, into exquisite abstractions, mathematics of emotion in place of the violent impact, the volcanic eruptions of fever, lust, and delight.

Irony. Now Rango was projecting himself out of this realm, and wanted action. No more time for the guitar which had ensorcelled her, no more time to visit the gypsies as he had once promised, no more time to sleep in the morning as she had been learning, or to acquire by osmosis his art of throwing off responsibilities, his self-indulgence, his recklessness. . . .

As they sat in the cafe, he condemned his past life. He was full of contrition for the wasted hours, the wasted energy, the wasted years. He wanted a more austere life, action and fulfillment.

Suddenly Djuna looked down at her coffee and her eyes filled with stinging tears; the tears of irony burn the skin more fiercely. She wept because she had aroused in Rango the desire to serve a purpose which was not hers, to live now for others when already he lived for Zora, and had so little to give her of himself. She wept because they were so close in that earthy darkness, close in the magnetic pull between their skin, their hair, their bodies, and yet their dreams never touched at any point, their vision of life, their attitudes. She wept over the many dislocations of life, forbidding the absolute unity.

Rango did not understand.

In the realm of ideas he was always restless, impatient, and like some wild animal who feared to be corralled. He often described how the horses, the bulls, were corralled in his ranch. He delighted in the fierceness of the battle. For him to examine, to understand, to interpret was exactly like some corralling activity, of which he was suspicious.

But for the moment, she was breathing the odor of his hair. For the moment there was this current between their skin and flesh, these harmonizations of contrasting colors, weight, quality, odors. Everything about him was pungent and violent. They were as his friends said, like Othello and Desdemona.

Mañana he would be a party member.

When you lose your wings, thought Djuna, this is the way you live. You buy candles for the meeting of Rango's friends, but these candles do not give a light that will delight you, because you do not believe in what you are doing.

Sadness never added to her weight; it caught her in flight as she danced in spirals misplacing air pools like an arrow shot at a bird which did not bring it down but merely increased its flutterings.

She had every day a greater reluctance to descend into familiar daily life, because the hurt, the huntsman's bow, came from the earth, and therefore flight at a safe distance became more and more imperative.

Her mobility was now her only defense against new dangers. While you're in movement it is harder to be shot at, to be wounded even. She had adopted the basic structure of the nomads.

Rango had said: "Prepare the barge for a meeting tonight. It will be an ideal place. No superintendents to tell tales to the police. No neighbors."

He had signed all the papers. They must be more careful.

The barge was being put to a greater usefulness.

There are two realms to live in now. (Do I hold the secret drug which permits me to hold on to the ecstasies while entering the life of the world, activities in the world, contingencies? I feel it coming to me while I am walking. It is a strange sensation, like drunkenness. It catches me in the middle of the street like a tremendous wave, and a numbness passes through my veins which is the numbness of the marvelous. I know it by its power, by the way it lifts my body, the air which passes under my feet. The cold room I left in the morning, the drab bedcovers, the stove full of ashes, the sour wine at the bottom of the glass were all illuminated by the force of love for Rango. It was as if I had learned to fly over the street and were permitted to do so for an instant . . . making every color more intense, every caress more penetrating, every moment more magnificent. . . . But I knew by the anxiety that it might not last. It is a state of grace of love, which some achieve by wine and others by prayer and fasting. It is a state of grace but I cannot discover what makes one fall out of it. The danger lies in flying low, in awakening. She knew she was flying lower now that Rango was to act in the world. The air of politics was charged with dust. People aspired to reach the planets, but it was a superfluous voyage; there was a certain way of breathing, of walking, of seeing, which transported human beings into space, into transparency. The extraordinary brilliancy of the games people played beyond themselves, the games of their starry selves. . . .)

She bought wood for the fire. She swept the barge. She concealed the bed and the barrel of wine.

Rango would guide the newcomers to the barge, and remain on the bridge to direct them.

The Guatemalans arrived gradually. The darker Indian-blooded ones in Indian silence, the paler Spanish-blooded ones with Spanish volubility. But both were intimidated by the place, the creaking wood, the large room resembling the early meeting places of the revolutionaries, the extended shadows, the river noises, chains, oars, the disquieting lights from the bridge, the swaying when other barges passed. Too much the place for conspirators. At times life surpasses the novel, the drama. This was one of them. The setting was more dramatic than they wished. They stood awkwardly around.

Rango had not yet come. He was waiting for those who were late.

Djuna did not know what to do. This was a role for which she had no precedent. Politeness or marginal talk seemed out of place. She kept the stove filled with wood and watched the flames as if her guardianship would make them active.

When you lose your wings, and wear a dark suit bought in the cheapest store of Paris, to become anonymous, when you discard your earrings, and the polish on your nails, hoping to express an abdication of the self, a devotion to impersonal service, and still you do not feel sincere, you feel like an actress, because you expect conversion to come like a miracle, by the grace of love for one party member. . . .

They know I am pretending.

That is how she interpreted the silence.

In her own eyes, she stood judged and condemned. She

was the only woman there, and they knew she was there only because she was a woman, tangled in her love, not in the revolution.

Then Rango came, breathless, and anxious: "There will be no meeting. You are ordered to disperse. No explanations."

They were relieved to go. They left in silence. They did not look at her.

Rango and Djuna were left alone.

Rango said: "*Your* friend the policeman was on guard at the top of the stairs. A hobo had been found murdered. So when the Guatemalans began to arrive, he asked for papers. It was dangerous." He had made his first error, in thinking the barge a good place. The head of the group had been severe. Had called him a romantic. . . . "He also knows about you. Asked if you were a member. I had to tell the truth."

"Should I sign the papers?" she asked, with a docility which was so much like a child's that Rango was moved.

"If you do it for me, that's bad. You have to do it for yourself."

"Oh, for myself. You know what I believe. The world today is rootless; it's like a forest with all the trees with their heads in the ground and their roots gesticulating wildly in the air, withering. The only remedy is to begin a world of two; in two there is hope of perfection, and that in turn may spread to all. . . . But it must begin at the base, in relationship of man and woman."

"I'm going to give you books to read, to study."

Would his new philosophy change his over-indulgence and slavishness to Zora, would he see her with new eyes, see the waste, the criminality of her self-absorption? Would he say to her, too: there are more important things in the world than your little pains. One must forget one's personal life. Would his personal life be altered as she had not been able to alter it? Would his confusions and errors be clarified?

Djuna began to hope. She began to study. She noted analogies between the new philosophy and what she had been expounding uselessly to Rango.

For instance, to die romantically, recklessly, unintelligently, was not approved by the party. Waste. Confusion. Indiscipline. The party developed a kind of stoicism, an armature, a form of behavior and thinking.

Djuna gradually allied herself to the essence of the

philosophy, to its results rather, and overlooked the rigid dogmas.

The essence was construction. In a large way she could adopt this because it harmonized with her obsessional battle against destruction and negativism.

She was not alone against the demoralizing, dissolving influence of Zora.

Perhaps the trap was opening a little, in an unforeseen direction.

What he could not do for her (because she was his pleasure, his self-indulgence, his sensually fulfilling mistress, and this gave him guilt), he might do for the party and for a large, anonymous mass of people.

The trap was the fixation on the impossible. A change in Zora, instead of an aggravation. A change in Rango, instead of a gradual strangulation.

Passion alone had not made him whole. But it had made him whole enough to be useful to the world.

When the barge failed to become the meeting place for Rango's fellow workers, it was suddenly transformed into its opposite: a shelter for the dreamers looking for a haven. The more bitter the atmosphere of Paris, the more intense the dissensions, the rising tide of political antagonisms, dangers, fears, the more they came to the barge as if it were Noah's Ark against a new deluge.

It was no longer the secret boat of a voyage of two. The unicellular nights had come to an end. Rango was but a visitor-lover in transit.

The divergence between them became sharply exteriorized: while Rango attended meetings, talked feverishly in cafes, sought to convert, to teach, to organize, worked among the poor he had known, among the artists, Djuna's friends brought to the barge the values they believed in danger of being lost, a passionate clinging to aesthetic and human creation.

Rango brought stories of cruelty and personal sacrifice: Ramon had been four years without seeing his wife and child. He had been working in Guatemala. Now his wife in Paris was gravely ill, and he wanted to throw off his duties there and come, at any cost. "Think of a man forgetting his loyalty to his party, just because his wife and child need him. Willing to sacrifice the good of millions, perhaps, for just two."

"Rango, that's just what you would do, and you know it. That's what you have done with Zora. You've given twenty years of your strength to one human being, when you could have done greater things, too. . . ."

Another day he came and was sick in her arms, vomited all night, and only at dawn, weak, and feverish did he confess: they had had to arrest a traitor. He had been a friend of Rango's. The group had been obliged to judge him. Rango had been forced to question him. The man was not really a traitor. He was weak. He had needed money for his family. He was tired of working for the party without pay. The party never worried about a man's family, what they needed while he was away on duty. He had given his whole life, and now, at forty, he had weakened. He had been tempted by a good position in the embassy. At first he had intended to exploit his position for the benefit of the party. But after a while he got tired of danger. He had ceased to be of help. . . . Rango had had to force himself to turn him over to the party. It had made him sick. It was his first cruel, difficult, disciplined act. But he didn't sleep for a week, and each time he remembered the man's face as he told his story, and repeated: just tired, very tired, worn out, at forty, too many times in prison, too many hardships, couldn't take any more. Had been in the party from the age of seventeen, had been useful, courageous, but now he was tired.

Every day he brought a story like this one. When the conflict grew too great he drank. Djuna did not have this escape. When the stories burnt into her and hurt her, she turned away and into the dream again, as she had done in childhood. There was another world visible to practiced eyes, easy to enter and inhabit, another chamber to which only the initiate could follow.

(Moods flowing like the river finding its way to the sea and vastness and depth. In this world the river was the flow; tap the secret of its flow, in the lulling rhythm of its waves, in the continuity of its current. Love is a madness shared by two, love is the crystal in which people find their unity. In this world Rango was capable of giving himself to a dream of love, which is a city of only two inhabitants. In this world, when Rango buys shoes so heavy and so strong, they seem like the hoofs of the centaur, hoofs of iron, whose head was in the heavens but whose hoofs must pound the battlefields.)

There are drugs to escape reality, a Rango vomiting from the spectacle of cruelty, Rango's harshness toward her feelings. He should, by laws of accuracy, be angry at his own emotionalism and human fallibility. But because of his blindness, he gets angry at Djuna's face turned away and attacks her swift departures from horror. He drinks but does not consider *that* a trap door opening on the infinite, an inferior drug to dispel pain. . . . But Djuna's excursions into astronomy, her sheltering of the artists in the barge . . . he is merciless toward their kind of drug to transform reality into something bearable. . . .

159

"To me, it is the world of history which appears mad, treacherous and full of contradictions," said Djuna.

"In Guatemala," said Rango, with an ironic twist of his lips which Djuna disliked, "they placed madmen by the side of the river, and that cured them. If your madmen don't get cured, we'll make a hole in the floor and sink them."

"I may sink with them, you know."

Walking along the quay, they saw a hobo sitting under a tree, a hobo with a Scotch cap, a plaid, and a crooked pipe.

Rango adopted his best imitation of a Scotch accent and said: "Weel, and where d'ya come from, ma good friend?"

But the hobo looked up bewildered and said in pure Montmartre French: "Mon Dieu, I'm no foreigner, sir. What makes you think I am?"

"The cap and the blanket," said Rango.

"Oh, that, sir, it's just that I'm always digging in the

garbage can of the Opéra Comique, and I found this rig. It was the only one I could wear, you understand, the others were a little too fancy, and most of them pretty indecent, I must say."

Then he took a faded gray sporran out of his pocket: "Could you tell me what this is for?"

Rango laughed: "That's a wig. The use of the skirt has caused premature baldness of an unusual kind in Scotland. Hold on to it, it might come useful one day. . . ."

Sabina walked with her feet flat on the ground, which gave to her heavy body the poise of Biblical water carriers.

Djuna saw her and Rango as composed of the same elements, and felt that perhaps they would love each other. She imagined a parting scene with Rango, surrendering his black hair to hers heavy and straight, his burnt-sienna skin to her incandescent gold one, his rough dry hands to her strong peasant ones, his laughter to hers, his Indian slyness to her Semitic labyrinthian mind. They will recognize each other's climate of fever and chaos, and embrace each other.

Djuna was amazed to see her predictions unfulfilled. Rango fled from Sabina's intensity and violence. They met like two armed warriors, and that part of Rango which longed to be yielded to, who longed for warmth, found in Sabina an unyielding armor. She yielded only at the last moment, merely to achieve a sensual embrace, and immediately after was poised for battle again. No aperture for tenderness to lodge itself, for his secret timidity to flow into, as it flew into Djuna's breast. Not a woman one could nestle into.

They sought grounds for a duel. Rango hated her presence about Djuna, and would have liked to drive her away from the barge.

Once sitting in a restaurant together, with Djuna and two other friends, they decided to see which one could eat the most red chilies.

They ate the red chilies with ostentatious insolence, watching each other. At first mixed with rice and vegetables, then with the salad, and finally by themselves.

Both might have died of the contest, for neither one would yield. Each little red chili like a concentrate of fire which burned them both.

Now and then they opened their mouth wide and breathed quickly in and out, as if to cool their insides.

As in the old myths, they sat like fire eaters partaking of a fire banquet. Tears came to Sabina's intense dark eyes. A sepia flush came to Rango's laughing cheeks, but neither would yield, though they might scar their entrails.

Fortunately the restaurant was closing, and the waiters maliciously washed the floor under their feet with ammonia, piled chairs on the table, and finally put an end to the marathon by turning out the lights.

Not one but many Djunas descended the staircase of the barge, one layer formed by the parents, the childhood, another molded by her profession and her friends, still another born of history, geology, climate, race, economics, and all the backgrounds and backdrops, the sky and nature of the earth, the pure sources of birth, the influence of a tree, a word dropped carelessly, an image seen, and all the corrupted sources: books, art, dogmas, tainted friendships, and all the places where a human being is wounded, defeated, crippled, and which fester. . . .

People add up their physical mishaps, the stubbed toes, the cut finger, the burn scar, the fever, the cancer, the microbe, the infection, the wounds and broken bones. They never add up the accumulated bruises and scars of the inner lining, forming a complete universe of reactions, a reflected world through which no event could take place without being subjected to a personal and private interpretation, through this kaleidoscope of memory, through the peculiar formation of the psyche's sensitive photographic plates, to this assemblage of emotional chemicals through which every word, every event, every experience is filtered, digested, deformed, before it is projected again upon people and relationships.

The movement of the many layers of the self described by Duchamp's Nude Descending a Staircase, the multiple selves grown in various proportions, not singly, not evenly developed, not moving in one direction, but composed of multiple juxtapositions revealing endless spirals of character as the earth revealed its strata, an infinite constellation of feelings expanding as mysteriously as space and light in the realm of the planets.

Man turned his telescope outward and far, not seeing character emerging at the opposite end of the telescope by subtle accumulations, fragments, accretions, and encrustations.

Woman turned her telescope to the near, and the warm.

Djuna felt at this moment a crisis, a mutation, a need to leap from the self born of her relationship to Rango and Zora, a need to resuscitate in another form. She was unable to follow Rango in his faith, unable either to live in the dream in peace, or to sail the barge accurately through a stormy Seine.

She found herself defending Sabina against Rango's ruthless mockery. She defended Sabina's philosophy of the many loves against the One.

(Rango, your anger should not be directed against Sabina. Sabina is ony behaving as all women do in their dreams, at night. I feel responsible for her acts, because when we walk together and I listen to her telling me about her adventures, a part of me is not listening to her telling me a story but recognizing scenes familiar to a secret part of myself. I recognize scenes I have dreamed and which therefore I have committed. What is dreamed is committed. In my dreams I have been Sabina. I have escaped from your tormenting love, caressed all the interchangeable lovers of the world. Sabina cannot be made alone responsible for acting the dreams of many women, just because the others sit back and participate with a secret part of their selves. Through secret and small vibrations of the flesh they admit being silent accomplices to Sabina's acts. At night we have all tossed with fever and desire for strangers. During the day we deride Sabina, and revile her. You're angry at Sabina because she lives out all her wishes overtly as you have done. To love Sabina's fever, Sabina's impatience, Sabina's evasion of traps in the games of love, was being Sabina. To be only at night what Sabina dared to be during the day, to bear the responsibility for one's secret dream of escape from the torments of one love into many loves.)

Sabina sat astride a chair, flinging her hair back with her hands and laughing.

She always gave at this moment the illusion that she was going to confess. She excelled in this preparation for unveiling, this setting of a mood for intimate revelations. She excelled equally in evasion. When she wished it, her life was like a blackboard on which she wrote swiftly and then erased almost before anyone could read what she had written. Her words then did not seem like words but like smoke issuing from her mouth and nostrils, a heavy smoke screen against detection. But at other times, if she felt secure from judgment, then she opened a story of an incident with direct, stabbing thoroughness. . . .

"Our affair lasted . . . lasted for the duration of an

elevator ride! And I don't mean that symbolically either! We took such a violent fancy to each other, the kind that will not last, but will not wait either. It was cannibalistic, and of no importance, but it had to be fulfilled once. Circumstances were against us. We had no place to go. We wandered through the streets, we were ravenous for each other. We got into an elevator, and he began to kiss me. . . . First floor, second floor, and he still kissing me, third floor, fourth floor, and when the elevator came to a standstill, it was too late . . . we could not stop, his hands were everywhere, his mouth. . . . I pressed the button wildly and went on kissing as the elevator came down. . . . When we got to the bottom it was worse . . . he pressed the button and we went up and down, up and down, madly, while people kept ringing for the elevator. . . ."

She laughed again, with her entire body, even her feet, marking the rhythm of her gaiety, stamping the ground like a delighted spectator, while her strong thighs rocked the chair like an Amazon's wooden horse.

One evening while Djuna was waiting for Rango at the barge, she heard a footstep which was not the watchman's and not Rango's.

The shadows of the candles on the tarpapered walls played a scene from a Balinese theatre as she moved toward the door and called: "Who's there?"

There was a complete silence, as if the river, the barge, and the visitor had connived to be silent at the same moment, but a tension in the air which she felt like a vibration through her body.

She did not know what to do, whether to stay in the room and lock the door, awaiting Rango, or to explore the barge. If she stayed in the room quietly and watched for his coming, she could shout a warning to him out of the window, and then together they might corner the intruder.

She waited.

The shadows on the walls were still, but the reflections of the lights on the river played on the surface like a ghost's carnival. The candles flickered more than usual, or was it her anxiety?

When the wood beams ceased to creak, she heard the footsteps again, moving toward the room, cautiously but not light enough to prevent the boards from creaking.

Djuna took her revolver from under her pillow, a small

one which had been given to her and which she did not know how to use.

She called out: "Who is there? If you come any nearer I'll shoot."

She knew there was a safety clasp to open. She wished Rango would arrive. He had no physical fear. He feared truth, he feared to confront his motives, feared to face, to understand, to examine in the realm of feelings and thought, but he did not fear to act, he did not fear physical danger. Djuna was intrepid in awareness, in painful exposures of the self, and dared more than most in matter of emotional surgery, but she had a fear of violence.

She waited another long moment, but again the silence was complete, suspended.

Rango did not come.

Out of exhaustion, she lay down with her revolver in hand. The doors and windows were locked. She waited, listening for Rango's uneven footsteps on the deck.

The candles burnt down one by one, gasping out their last flame, throwing one last long, agonized skeleton on the wall.

The river rocked the barge.

Hours passed and Djuna fell into a half sleep.

The catch of the door was gradually lifted off the hinge

by some instrument or other and Zora stood at the opened door.

Djuna saw her when she was bending over her, and screamed.

Zora held a long old-fashioned hatpin in her hand and tried to stab Djuna with it. Djuna at first grasped her hands at the wrists, but Zora's anger gave her greater strength. Her face was distorted with hatred. She pulled her hands free and stabbed at Djuna several times blindly, striking her at the shoulder, and then once more, with her eyes wide open, she aimed at the breast and missed. Then Djuna pushed her off, held her.

"What harm have I done you, Zora?"

"You forced Rango to join the party. He's trying to become someone now, in politics, and it's for you. He wants you to be proud of him. With me he never cared; he wasn't ashamed of his laziness. . . . It's your fault that he is never home . . . your fault that he's in danger every day."

Djuna looked at Zora's face and felt again as she did with Rango, the desperate hopelessness of talking, explaining, clarifying. Zora and Rango were fanatics.

She shook Zora by the shoulders, as if to force her to listen and said: "Killing me won't change anything, can't you understand that? We're the two faces of Rango's character. If you kill me, that side of him remains unmated and another woman will take my place. He's divided within himself, between destruction and construction. While he's divided there will be two women, always. I wished you would die, too, once, until I understood this. I once thought Rango could be saved if you died. And here you are, thinking that I would drive him into danger. He's driving himself into danger. He is ashamed of his futility. He can't bear the conflict of his split being enacted in us before his eyes. He is trying a third attempt at wholeness. For his peace of mind, if you and I could have been friends it would have been easier. He didn't consider us, whether or not we could sincerely like each other. We tried and failed. You were too selfish. You and I stand at opposite poles. I don't like you, and you don't like me either; even if Rango did not exist you and I could never like each other. Zora, if you harm me you'll be punished for it and sent to a place without Rango. . . . And Rango will be angry with you. And if you died, it would be the same, he would not be mine either, because I can't fulfill his love of destruction. . . ."

Words, words, words . . . all the words Djuna had turned in her mind at night when alone, she spoke them wildly, blindly, not hoping for Zora to understand, but

they were said with such anxiety and vehemence that aside from their meaning Zora caught the pleading, the accents of truth, dissolving her hatred, her violence.

At the sight of each other their antagonism always dissolved. Zora, faced with the sadness of Djuna's face, her voice, her slender body, could never sustain her anger. And Djuna faced with Zora's haggard face, limp hair, uncontrolled lips, lost her rebellion.

Whatever scenes took place between them, there was a sincerity in each one's sadness which bound them, too.

It was at this moment that Rango arrived, and stared at the two women with dismay.

"What happened? Djuna, you're bleeding!"

"Zora tried to kill me. The wounds aren't bad."

Djuna hoped once more that Rango would say, "Zora is mad," and that the nightmare would cease.

"You wanted us to be friends, because that would have made it easier for you. We tried. But it was impossible. I feel that Zora destroys all my efforts to create with you, and she thinks I sent you into a dangerous political life. . . . We can never understand each other."

Rango found nothing to say. He stared at the blood showing through Djuna's clothes. She showed him that the stabs were not deep and had struck fleshy places without causing harm.

"I'll take Zora home. I'll come back."

When he returned he was still silent, crushed, bowed.

"Zora has moments of madness," he said. "She's been threatening people in the street lately. I'm so afraid the police may catch her and put her in an institution."

"You don't care about the people she might kill, do you?"

"I do care, Djuna. If she had killed you I don't think I could ever have forgiven her. But you aren't angry, when you have a right to be. You're generous and good. . . ."

"No, Rango. I can't let you believe that. It isn't true. I have often wished Zora's death, but I only had the courage to wish it. . . . I had a dream one night in which I saw myself killing her with a long old-fashioned hatpin. Do you realize where she got the idea of the hatpin? From my own dream, which I told her. She was being more courageous, more honest, when she attacked me."

Rango took his head in his hands and swayed back and forth as if in pain. A dry sob came out of his chest.

"Oh, Rango, I can't bear this any more. I will go away. Then you'll have peace with Zora."

"Something else happened today, Djuna, something which reminded me of some of the things you said. Something so terrible that I did not want to see you tonight. I don't know what instinct of danger made me come, after all. But what happened tonight is worse than Zora's fit of madness. You know that once a month the workers of the party belonging to a certain group meet for what they call autocriticism. It's part of the discipline. It's done with kindness, great objectivity, and very justly. I have been at such meetings. A man's way of working, his character traits, are analyzed. Last night it was my turn. The men who sat in a circle, they were the ones I see every day, the butcher, the postman, the grocer, the shoemaker on my own street. The head of our particular section is the bus driver. At first, you know, they had been doubtful about signing me in. They knew I was an artist, a bohemian, an intellectual. But they liked me . . . and they took me in. I've worked for them two months now. Then last night. . . ."

He stopped as if he would not have the courage to re-live the scene. Djuna's hand in his calmed him. But he kept his head bowed. "Last night they talked, very quietly and moderately as the French do. . . . They analyzed me, how I work. They told me some of the things you used to tell me. They made an analysis of my character. They observed everything, the good and the bad. Not only the laziness, the disorder, the lack of dis-cipline, the placing of personal life before the needs of the party, the nights at the cafe, the immoderate talking, irresponsibility, but they also mentioned my capabilities, which made it worse, as they showed how I sabotage myself. . . . They analyzed my power to influence others, my eloquence, my fervor and enthusiasm, my contagious enthusiasm and energy, my gift for making an impression on a crowd, the fact that people are inclined to trust me, to elect me as their leader. Everything. They knew about my fatalism, too. They talked about character changing, as you do. They even intimated that Zora should be placed in an institution, because they knew about her behavior."

All the time he kept his head bowed.

"When you said these things gently, it didn't hurt me. It was our secret and I could get angry with you, or contradict you. But when they said them before all the other men I knew it was true, and worse still, I knew that if I had not been able to change with all that you gave me, years of love and devotion, I wouldn't change for the party either. . . . Any other man, taking what you gave, would have accomplished the greatest changes . . . any other man but me."

The barge was sailing nowhere, moored to the port of despair.

Rango stretched himself and said: "I'm tired out . . . so tired, so tired. . . ." And fell asleep almost instantly in the pose of a big child, with his fists tightly closed, his arms over his head.

Djuna walked lightly to the front cabin, looked once through the small barred portholes like the windows of a prison, leaned over the mildewed floor, and tore up one of the bottom boards, inviting the deluge to sink this Noah's Ark sailing nowhere.

The wood being old and half rotted had made it easy for Djuna to pull on the plank where it had once been patched, but the influx of the water had been partly blocked by the outer layer of barnacles and corrugated seaweeds which she could not reach.

She returned to the bed on the floor and lay beside Rango, to wait patiently for death.

She saw the river sinuating toward the sea and wondered if they would float unhampered toward the ocean.

Below the level of identity lay an ocean, an ocean of which human beings carry only a drop in their veins; but some sink below cognizance and the drop becomes a huge wave, the tide of memory, the undertows of sensation. . . .

Beneath the cities of the interior flowed many rivers carrying a multitude of images. . . .

All the women she had been spread their hair in a halo on the surface of the river, extended multiple arms like the idols of India, their essence seeping in and out of the meandering dreams of men. . . .

Djuna, lying face upward like a water lily of ammiotic lakes; Djuna, floating down to the organ grinder's tune of a pavana for a defunct infanta of Spain, the infanta who never acceded to the throne of maturity, the one who remained a pretender. . . .

As for Rango, the drums would burst and all the painted horses of the carnival would turn a polka. . . .

She saw their lives over and over again until she caught a truth which was not simple and divisible but fluctuating and elusive; but she saw it clearly from the places under the surface where she had been accustomed to exist: all the women she had been like many rivers running out of her and with her into the ocean. . . .

She saw, through this curtain of water, all of them as personages larger than nature, more visible to sluggish hearts being in the focus of death, a stage on which there are no blurred passages, no missed cues. . . .

She saw, now that she was out of the fog of imprecise relationships, with the more intense light of death upon these faces which had caused her despair, she saw these same faces as pertaining to gentle clowns. Zora dressed in comical trappings, in Rango's outsized socks, in dyed kimonos, in strangled rags and empty-armed brooches, a comedy to awaken guilt in others. . . .

. . . on this stage, floating down the Seine toward death, the actors drifted along and love no longer seemed a trap *. . . the trap was the static pause in growth, the arrested self caught in its own web of obstinacy and obsession.* . . .

. . . you grow, as in the water the algae grow taller and heavier and are carried by their own weight into different currents. . . .

. . . I was afraid to grow or move away, Rango, I was ashamed to desert you in your torment, but now I know your choice is your own, as mine was my own. . . .

. . . fixation is death . . . death is fixation. . . .

. . . on this precarious ship, devoid of upholstery and self-deception, the voyage can continue into tomorrow. . . .

. . . what I see now is the vastness, and the places where I have not been and the duties I have not fulfilled, and the uses for this unusual cargo of past sorrows all ripe for transmutations. . . .

. . . the messenger of death, like all adventurers, will accelerate your heart toward change and mutation. . . .

. . . if one sinks deep enough and then deeper, all these women she had been flowed into one at night and lost their separate identities; she would learn from Sabina how to make love laughing, and from Stella how to die only for a little while and be born again as children die and are reborn at the slightest encouragement. . . .

. . . from the end in water to the beginning in water, she would complete the journey, from origin to birth and birth to flow. . . .

. . . she would abandon her body to flow into a vaster body than her own, as it was at the beginning, and return with many other lives to be unfolded. . . .

. . . with her would float the broken doll of her childhood, the Easter egg which had been smaller than the one she had asked for, debris of fictions. . . .

. . . she would return to the life above the waters of the unconscious and see the magnifications of sorrow which had taken place and been the true cause of the deluge. . . .

. . . there were countries she had not yet seen. . . .

. . . this image created a pause in her floating. . . .

. . . there must also be loves she had not yet encountered. . . .

. . . as the barge ran swiftly down the current of despair, she saw the people on the shore flinging their arms in desolation, those who had counted on her Noah's Ark to save themselves. . . .

. . . she was making a selfish journey. . . .

. . . she had intended the barge for other purposes than for a mortuary. . . .

. . . war was coming. . . .

. . . the greater the turmoil, the confusion, the greater had been her effort to maintain an individually perfect world, a cocoon of faith, which would be a symbol and a refuge. . . .

. . . the curtain of dawn would rise on a deserted river . . . on two deserters. . . .

. . . in the imminence of death she seized this intermediary region of our being in which we rehearse our future sorrows and relive the past ones. . . .

. . . in this heightened theatre their lives appeared in their true color because there was no witness to distort the private admissions, the most absurd pretensions. . . .

. . . in the last role Djuna became immune from the passageway of pretense, from a suspended existence in reflection, from impostures. . . .

. . . and she saw what had appeared immensely real to her as charades. . . .

. . . . *on the theatre of death, exaggeration is the cause of despair.* . . .

. . . the red Easter egg I had wanted to be so enormous when I was a child, if it floats by today in its natural size, so much smaller than my invention, I will be able to laugh at its shrinking. . . .

. . . I had chosen death because I was ashamed of this shrinking and fading, of what time would do to our fiction of magnificence, time like the river would wear away the pain of defeats and broken promises, time and the river would blur the face of Zora as a giant incubus, time and the river would mute the vibrations of Rango's voice upon my heart. . . .

. . . the organ grinder will play all the time but it will not always seem like a tragic accompaniment to separations. . . .

. . . the organ grinder will play all the time but the images will change, as the feelings will change, Rango's gestures will seem less violent, and sorrows will fall off like leaves to fecundate the heart for a new love. . . .

. . . the organ grinder will accelerate his rhythm into arabesques of delight to match the vendor's cries: "Mimosa! mimosa!" to the tune of Grieg's Sleep, My Little Angel, Sleep.

. . . "Couteaux! couteaux à éguiser!" to the tune of Madame Butterfly.

. . . *"Pommes de terre! pommes de terre!"* to the tune of Ravel's Bolero.

. . . *"Bouteilles! bouteilles!"* to the tune of Tristam and Iseult.

She laughed.

. . . tomorrow the city would ferment with new disasters, the paper vendors would raise their voices to the pitch of hysteria, the crowds would gather to discuss the news, the trains would carry away the cowards. . . .

. . . the cowards. . . .

. . . floating down the river. . . .

. . . with the barge that had been intended not only to house a single love but as a refuge for faith. . . .

. . . she was sinking a faith. . . .

. . . instead of solidifying the floating kingdom with its cargo of eternal values. . . .

("An individually perfect world," said Rango, "is destroyed by reality, war, revolutions.")

"Rango, wake up wake up wake up, there's a leak!"

He was slow in awakening, his dreams of greatness and magnificence were heavy on his body like royal garments, but the face he opened to the dawn was the face of innocence, as every man presents innocence to the new day. Djuna read on it what she had refused to see, the other face of Rango the child lodged in a big man's body by a merry freak.

It had been a game: "Djuna, you stand there and watch while I am the king and savior. You will admire me when I give the cue." She will now laugh and say: "But actually, you know, I prefer a hobo who plays the guitar."

She will laugh when he refuses to see Zora's madness, because it was like her refusal to see his madness, his impersonations, his fictions, his illusions. . . .

In the face of death the barge was smaller, Rango did not loom so immense, Zora had shrunk. . . .

In the face of death they were playing games, Zora absurdly overdressed in the trappings of tragedy, muddying, aborting, confusing, delighted with the purple colors of catastrophe as children delight in fire engines. When their absence of wisdom and courage tormented her, she would avenge herself by descending into their realm and adding to the difficulties. She had once told Rango that her father would have to live in the south of France for his health and that they would have to separate. Being helpless, they had believed she would let this happen, since they were accustomed to bowing to the inevitable. Rango had jumped and leaped with pain. Zora had said to him, not without mixing it with a delicate shading of poison: "This must happen sooner or later . . . Djuna will leave you."

Then she had gone to see Zora, Zora awkwardly, laboriously moving her small and flabby hands, Zora appearing helpless while Djuna knew she was the strongest of the three because she had learned to exploit her weakness. She told Djuna that Rango had not eaten that day. He was just pacing around, and he had been so cruel to Zora. He had said to her: "If Djuna goes to the south of France, I'll send you home to your relatives."

"Alone? And what about you?"

"Oh, me," he said with a shrug. Zora added: "He will kill himself."

By this time her game had given her enough pleasure. She felt mature again. But after a week of torment the stage was set for a great love scene; she knew now that if she left Rango he would not console himself with Zora. That was all she needed to know. Perhaps she was not so much wiser than they were . . . perhaps she did not have herself too great a faith in love. . . . Perhaps there was in her a Zora in need of protection and a wildly anxious Rango in need of reassurances. And perhaps that was why she loved them, and perhaps Zora was right to believe in her love as she did in her moments of lucidity. . . .

In the face of death Rango seemed less violent, Zora less tyrannical, and Djuna less wise. And when Zora looked at Djuna above the rim of her glasses which she had picked up in a scrap basket at somebody's door and which were not suited to her eyes—she looked as children do when they stare and frown over the rim of their parents' glasses, these pretenders to the throne of maturity. . . .

"Rango, wake up wake up wake up wake up wake up, there's a leak."

Rango opened his eyes and then jumped: "Oh, I forgot to pump the water yesterday."

The second face of Rango, after awakening, following the bewildered and innocent one, contained this expression of total, of absolute, distress common to children and adolescents betraying an exaggeration in the vision of reality, a sense of the menacing, disproportionate stature of this reality. Only children and adolescents know this total despair, as if every wound were fatal and irremediable, every moment the last, death and dangers looming immense as they had loomed in Djuna's mind during the night. . . .

Rango repaired the leak vigorously, and they walked out on the quay. It was a moment before dawn, and some fishermen were already installed because the river was smooth for fishing. One of them had caught something unusual and was holding it out for Djuna to see, and laughing.

It was a doll.

It was a doll who had committed suicide during the night. The water had washed off its features. Her hair aureoled her face with crystalline glow.

Noah's Ark had survived the flood.